I0838656
Fatal Kiss

Fatal Kiss

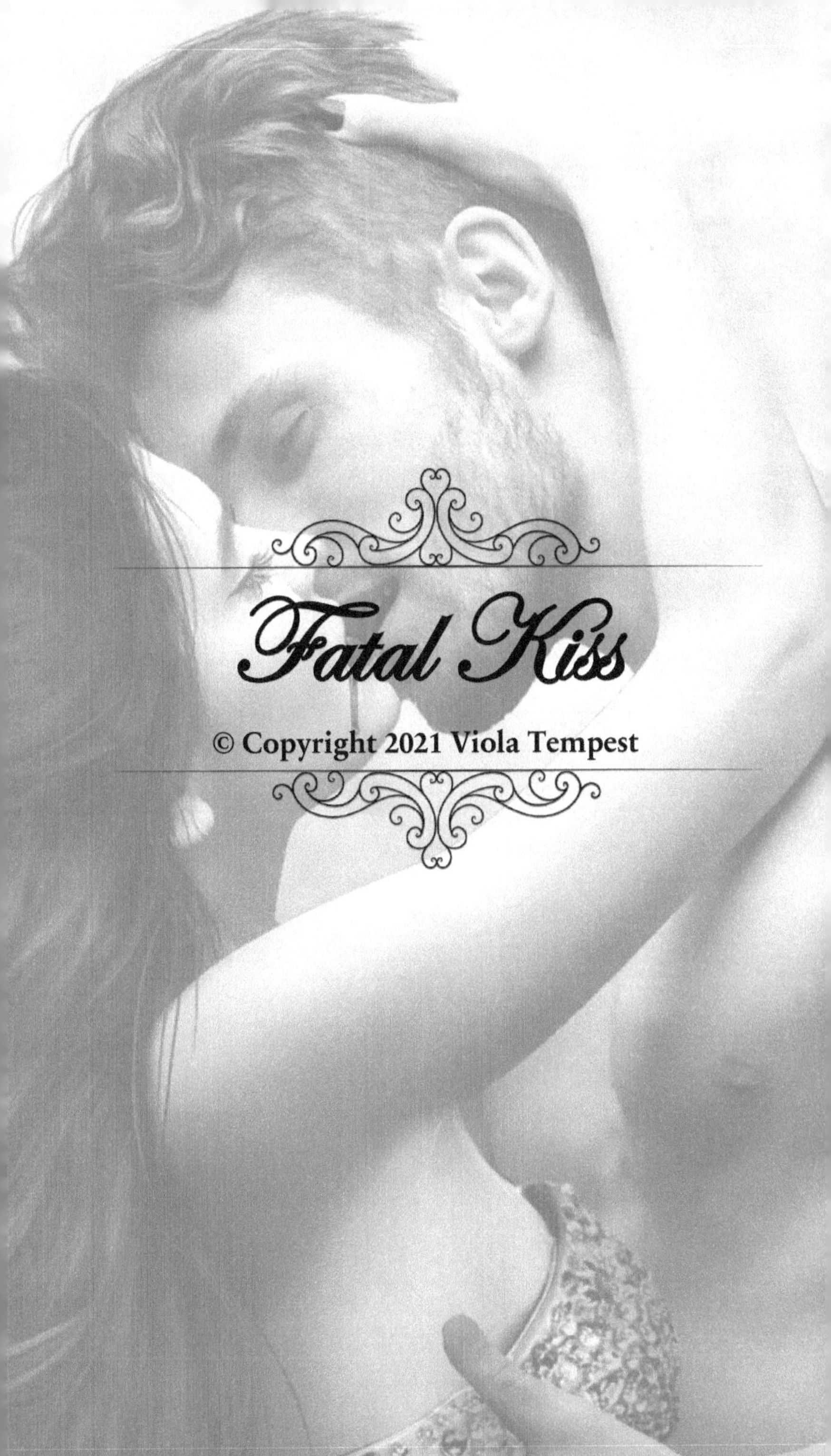

Fatal Kiss

© Copyright 2021 Viola Tempest

Any references to historical events, real people, or real places are used fictitiously. Names, characters, and places are products of the author's imagination.

Cover Design by Amanda Pillar
(Smoking Hot Covers)

Table of Contents

Table of Contents

Table of Contents

Chapter One

Geneva Beck tapped her pencil against her lip, feigning deep thought. Her skin tingled with a thirst for blood, but there was something acrid about the conversation in the room that made her lose her appetite.

Her last patient of the day, Felix Hart, was a Vietnam veteran and war hero who had lost his son in a car accident a few years ago. The subsequent strain it had caused on his relationship with his wife led them to couples counseling, where Geneva met them both.

Only now, just Felix remained. His wife passed not long after his son, leaving him to deal with the burden of grief alone. With both his wife and his son gone, Felix was a dithering mess. His eyes were soppy, his skin pallid and papery. There was a perpetual look of horror on his face that Geneva doubted went away even when he was sleeping.

She didn't want to admit how disgusted she was by the sight of his blubbering. Often, Geneva had to fight the urge to feed on even her patients, to use their blood to quell the unquenchable, fiery thirst of vampirism in her. But Felix was something else. She couldn't imagine how grotesque his pitiful blood would taste on her tongue.

"Dr. Beck, how do you do it?" Felix asked, his voice warbling with unfettered emotion. "How do you fill that void in your soul? I just don't see how I can be whole again without my wife and son."

Geneva refrained a roll of her eyes. It was a pity she found him so repulsive, or she might have just put him out of his misery and drained the blood from his body.

"There is no void, Felix," Geneva insisted. "You were whole before you met your wife or had your son, and you're still whole now."

Felix shook his head. "But I'm *not* whole, though," he argued. "All this loss and trauma have burned a hole through my soul."

He buried his face in his hands and heaved a long, watery sigh into his palms. As he collected his composure, Geneva watched him with detached interest.

"Perhaps, you're too young to understand," Felix suggested.

Inwardly, Geneva scoffed. As a vampire, she's undoubtedly lived a much more intense life than Felix had. She's experienced levels of trauma he could only dream of, which was part of what made her such a good psychologist. Though she was admittedly young, she had a long time to study the human psyche and analyze their behavior.

"I've experienced my fair share of trauma, Felix," she said, trying to keep the weariness from her tone.

It got harder and harder each day for her to put up a front for her patients, to pretend to care about their problems.

Just a few short years ago, she had gone to her usual watering hole after work to unwind. There, she met a man more handsome than she had ever seen, someone dark and mysterious, with an intriguing allure behind his mystifying eyes.

What she thought was supposed to be a one-night stand with an attractive stranger turned out to be something much different. That was the night she had been bitten, claimed by the two fang marks that still marred the skin at the junction of her neck and shoulder. Only one was visible above the collar of her shirt, looking as innocent as a birthmark.

That night had changed her forever. The way she had woken up in her empty bed, her blood thick and slow as it pumped through her. At first, she believed she was merely hung over. Her head pounded, and her heart raced. Soon, she became so sensitive to sunlight that she wore long sleeves and a brimmed hat even in the swelter of summer.

When she felt that first inkling of blood lust, she knew what had happened to her. The fang marks didn't lie, though they healed quickly. It was the compelling desire to bite into the tender flesh of other humans that confirmed it for her.

Most women might have been horrified, but Geneva thought her vampirism was the best thing to ever happen to her. She was stronger, immortal, and more cognizant than she had ever been.

It didn't come completely without a cost, though. Geneva was still very new to this, still learning to battle with her bloodlust and violent impulses. Over the years, she had slain many men, feeding exclusively on her paramours. There was something more appealing about their blood, about the heat and tension between them, that sweetened their taste and filled her belly in such a satisfying way.

But dead men could not love her, and she could not love dead men. Resisting the temptation to bite into their flesh got harder each time. She couldn't really even say that she had ever loved any of these men, only obsessed over them, only using their affections for her to sweeten their blood and give her a satisfying meal.

To say that she had experienced her fair share of trauma was an understatement. Geneva was the living embodiment of her trauma.

"How do you deal with it?" Felix asked, breaking her out of her reminiscent thoughts.

Geneva blinked at him, running her tongue over her sharp teeth. She shouldn't have been irritated by such a simple question. It was the whole reason he had come to her, after all.

But she was annoyed all the same because she couldn't think of a suitable answer – at least, not for *her* problems.

"Be patient, Felix," she said calmly. "You just need a little more time to heal."

Felix shook his head. "The *void*, Dr. Beck," he insisted. "Pretending it isn't there won't make it go away. What can I do to feel whole again?"

She wasn't sure that she had ever felt whole, so she had no idea what to say. She was growing more frustrated with him by the second.

"Acknowledge that the void isn't real," she insisted. "Stop trying to fill it. You're letting your loneliness speak for you."

Felix slowly heaved himself up to his feet and dusted off his khakis. "Dr. Beck, I appreciate you taking the time to see me today, but I think I may want to get a second opinion," he said. "I can't trust you to help me with my life when you've got a bigger hole in your heart than I do."

He walked to the door, sparing one last glance at her over his shoulder. Geneva watched him with her teeth clenched, itching to snap his neck and drain his blood, not even to drink, but just to see the crimson stain it left on her carpet.

"Take care of yourself, Dr. Beck."

Geneva's fingers were trembling when she finally left work. A few more emails and a final phone call were enough to get her out the door for the evening. After dealing with Felix's appointment, she was in desperate need of some reprieve. Her stomach was growling, but she didn't feel like dealing with the hassle of finding a suitable victim.

Instead, she wandered down to the pier just a short walk from her office. The sun was just starting to dip below the horizon, and a thick fog encroached from the turbulent ocean. A few years ago, she would have found this place a little too unsettling to make herself comfortable. Now, she enjoyed that the eerie evening fog kept passersby in their homes. Only a fool would come out on a night like this, with the winds whipping and the tide pulling out.

She settled down on the edge of the pier, pulling off her black pumps so she can dip her toes into the frigid water. The waves lapped roughly against the shore, spraying her with a fine mist of salt water. Geneva didn't mind. There was something refreshing about the ocean, like it was doing its best to cleanse her.

The roar of the ocean waves was soothing, the fog like a comforting blanket. This weather was a curse for most humans, but for a monster like Geneva, it was a blessing. The sun could not accost her like it usually did, shrouded in the billowing dark nature around her. To her, it was as blissful as lying on a sunny beach.

Her phone rang, shattering the silent peace with its piercing shrill. Geneva sighed as she fished in her purse and pulled out her cell phone. Her sister's name flashed across the screen. As much as she loved her sister, she wasn't in the mood to talk to her now. Her family was blissfully unaware of her vampirism, and the more at arm's distance she kept them, the longer she could keep it like that.

Part of her *did* worry that as they began to age, and she didn't, they would notice. One day, she would have to leave this town and start a new life somewhere else.

That was too dark a place to let her mind drift, so Geneva reluctantly answered the call.

"Hey, Eugenia," she said, holding her phone against her ear with her shoulder so she could tie her hair up into a long ponytail.

"Geneva," her sister's voice crackled over the static. "I haven't heard from you in a while. Are you doing alright?"

"I'm good," Geneva replied. She was anything but good, but she had always been an exceptional liar.

"Well, I miss you, Eugenia said. "Parker is having a dinner party this weekend, and we both want you to come."

Geneva rolled her eyes. Her sister's husband, Parker Kim, was a sniveling, pathetic man, the kind of stuffed shirt tax attorney she would never give a second glance to. She could not, for the life of her, understand what her sister saw in him.

"Please, Geneva," she begged. "His sister and brother-in-law will be there, and I'd love for you to meet them. I think it would be good for you to have a friend in town, and I'm sure you'll get along well with his sister."

The wind whipped Geneva's ponytail around the back of her head as she stared out into the raging ocean. The tide was receding, baring the sharp rocks below – a lethal fall for a human, but not for Geneva. *It might hurt*, she thought as she peered over the edge, but she'd survive.

"I don't need your help to make friends, Eugenia," Geneva chided.

"I know. I just think you'd like her."

Geneva pursed her lips together. She let a brief silence crackle over the line, unsure of what to say. Eugenia wasn't the only one in her family to remark on her absence of lovers or friends. She could never escape that judgement.

"So, do you think you can come?" Eugenia asked. "Please, Geneva. I'd love it if you could be there. It's been so long since we hung out."

With heavy reluctance, Geneva agreed. "Of course, I'll come, Eugenia," she said. "If it'll make you happy."

Eugenia squealed, causing the static feedback to make Geneva wince and pull her ear away from the phone. "Thank you, Geneva," she gushed. "I'll make that shrimp scampi Parker's mom gave me the recipe for. I know you'll love it."

Geneva listened to her chatter, faintly amused. There were few people she cared as much about as her sister, and fortunately for Geneva, it was fairly simple to make her happy. As the older of the two, Geneva had always felt responsible for Eugenia, though from an outside perspective, Eugenia was the one with her life together.

"You know, you can bring a date," Eugenia suggested, her voice cautious. "If you want to. I think you should, though. I mean, you'll stand out like a sore thumb if you come alone, so maybe, it would be best to bring someone along."

"Eugenia!" Geneva snapped. "Why are you always doing this to me?"

"Doing what to you?" Eugenia demanded. "I'm not doing anything. I just want to see my big sister happy. Is that so wrong?"

"You don't want to see me happy. You want to see me with a man."

"Isn't that what *you* want?" Eugenia asked. "You were literally obsessed with every boyfriend you've ever had. I just don't understand why you refuse to date anyone now. You used to be so boy crazy!"

Geneva rolled her eyes again. "I wasn't boy crazy."

"Well, I don't know what else you can call it," Eugenia retorted. "Listen, if you don't want to bring a date, that's up to you. I'm not going to force you. I still want you to come regardless."

"I'll think about it."

Eugenia murmured her acknowledgement, though Geneva knew she already suspected she wouldn't let it go. They said their goodbyes and hung up. Geneva resisted the strong urge to chuck her phone into the ocean.

Chapter Two

The sun had dipped all the way beneath the horizon, casting an ethereal darkness over the pier. Her sights were more attuned than humans, and she could still see easily in spite of the thick fog and settling darkness. She looked down to the jagged rocks below and shivered.

With her heightened sense of hearing, she detected the sound of soft footsteps behind her. They were maybe thirty feet away but approaching her in a straight path. Her hackles were raised as the footsteps neared, but she feigned ignorance and leaned back against the dock. The wood was damp and giving beneath her fingers, the scent of salt air invading her senses.

When the footsteps stopped, she waited with bated breath.

"The pier is closed," said the rich rumble of a man's voice.

Geneva turned her head just far enough to look at him, to gauge if he was a threat to her in any way.

Like most men she had met, she could immediately tell that he wasn't. She sensed nothing lethal about his blood, no sharp tang of vampirism or other night creatures on him. Yet, the sight of him still stopped her heart.

She had never seen a man so obtrusively attractive. Even in the dark, she could see the piercing green ice of his eyes, the sweep of dark curls across his forehead. He had a strong jaw, aristocratic features that reminded her of the dukes on regency romance novel covers. Somehow, his muddied fishing waders and tattered shirt did nothing to detract from his handsomeness. It was so pervading that Geneva felt the need to fully turn her head to drink him in.

Her nose wrinkled at him in feigned disgust. Part of her was a bit repulsed by his state of dress, but she easily overlooked it when he stepped closer, stabbing her with his steely gaze.

"I said, the pier is closed," he repeated, a stern set to his stubborn jaw. "There's a storm rolling in. It'll blow your tiny body right into the ocean, down onto those rocks."

Geneva repressed a shiver at the sound of his voice. He had a low, silky resonance to his tone, so rich and smooth she wanted to drink it.

"I'll take my chances," she said, turning her back to him so she could face the ocean again.

His footsteps came closer until he was standing beside her. Through her peripheral vision, she caught sight of his rubber, green boots.

"You're pretty brave to be out here by yourself in the dark. Hell, most people won't even come here alone during the day," he ventured, taking a seat on the edge of the dock. He threw his legs over the side and let them dangle beside Geneva's. "Not exactly dressed for the weather either. Don't tell me you came out here on a suicide mission. I'm more than qualified to talk you down, so don't even try it."

She scoffed and gave him a demure glance through her lashes. "How are you more than qualified?" she demanded.

"When I'm not saving pretty women from certain death, I'm a psychologist," he said. "I'm only joking, though. If I thought you were suicidal, I wouldn't joke about it."

She looked at him with suspicion, feeling a sudden and overwhelming thirst for blood. There was an open cut somewhere on his body; she could smell the coppery tang so potently in the night air. He was a perfect specimen, too, a handsome stranger, alone in the dark. He smelled enticingly sweet, but she knew he could taste even sweeter.

"A psychologist?" she asked. "I'm a psychologist, too."

He gave her a look of pleasant surprise, his eyes glinting. "That explains your clothes, then," he said, gesturing to her thin black pencil skirt.

She gave a coy shrug. "And what explains yours?"

He returned a sly shrug of his own. "Fishing?" he asked teasingly, "I work in the next town over, but I drive up here sometimes in the evenings after work to fish."

The wind around them began to pick up, and Geneva saw him shiver beneath his thin cotton shirt.

She didn't have the same compulsion to shiver, but she faked one anyway and crossed her arms over her chest.

"I guess you didn't check the weather this time," she said.

He let out a low chuckle. "No, I guess I didn't."

A comfortable silence settled over the pier. Geneva snuck glances at him as they let the winds and salty sea air roll over them. When a gentle mist of rain began to fall, Geneva slithered herself closer to him under the guise of seeking warmth.

"We should get out of here," he said. "The storm will hit soon."

"I think I'd like to stay," she insisted, enjoying the cool sprinkle of droplets on her skin.

The man gave her a curious look, his head tilted to the side. "What's your name?" he asked her.

He had a confidence about him that intrigued her. Many men were intimidated by her, but she supposed she didn't look as harrowing with her windswept hair and damp dress.

"Geneva Beck," she replied.

"Geneva Beck," he repeated. "A beautiful name. I'm Luke. Luke Mason."

He extended his arm for a handshake. Geneva gave him a dubious look before she slipped her fingers beside his and gave his palm a solid shake. He had large, warm hands, his grip firm but not too tight around hers.

Quickly, she pulled her hand away, back into the safety of her lap. His touch awakened the thirst in her, and she had already decided. She was hungry, and Luke would be her next victim. It was the perfect opportunity. She had always preferred the musky taste of men, especially the ones as attractive and muscular as Luke. He would be delicious once she prepped his blood with teasing flirtations and enthusiastic affections.

"Are you sure you don't want to go inside, Geneva?" he asked. There was a light and teasing tone to his voice, like he was amused at her expense. It sent an illicit thrill down her spine. "The fishery is just a short walk from here. We could wait out the storm in there, if you're so insistent to stay at the pier."

Geneva tossed him a dry look. "*You* can go wait out the storm in the fishery," she said. "*I'm* going to stay here and bask in nature's fury."

Luke let out a bark of laughter, a sound that carried even beneath the growing rage of the rain. "Bask in nature's fury?" he asked incredulously.

"Maybe you're more suicidal than I previously thought."

"I'm not suicidal," she insisted. Even if she were, a raging storm was not nearly enough of a force to end her life.

"Well, that's good," he said. "A suicidal psychologist can't be all that trustworthy."

Geneva was basically dead anyway. She didn't think vampiric psychologists were any less trustworthy, but she had never thought of herself as that kind of person. She was admittedly more selfish than that.

"Are *you* a trustworthy psychologist?" she asked. It felt important to know what kind of man he thought he was.

He gave an indifferent shrug. "I wouldn't be comfortable working if I didn't feel like I was trustworthy," he said, "but I am human. I'm as susceptible to making mistakes as just about anyone else. I do my best to take care of my patients. My clinic is reputable, so I have faith that I'm doing a decent job."

She peered closer at him, taking in the limp way his damp curls hung on his head, the pleasant lift at the corners of his mouth. He wore a faint grin, like he was modestly proud but too shy to confess the true magnitude of his success.

"What do you specialize in?" she asked, curious about him now that it seemed like he was holding back from her.

"Phobias and anxiety," he replied, leaning back against the dock.

The rain was falling in heavy sheets now, taking them from damp to drenched in a matter of seconds. Geneva watched him glance to the Eastern side of the pier where the fishery was. The storm was enough to make him uncomfortable, if not scared. She enjoyed seeing the flittering emotions on his face, the nervousness and fear that she could only catch small glimpses of.

"What about you?" he asked when she gave him no response.

Her gaze flicked back to his eyes, so vibrantly green that they seemed to swarm with life, like a lush biome residing in the swirls of malachite.

"Relationship counseling," she answered, keeping her eyes locked onto his.

She wanted to see every nuance to his reaction, to soak up whatever emotions will bleed from him throughout this titillating conversation.

"How interesting," he said, reaching for her left hand and lifting it close to his face. Geneva's heart hammered at the sensation of his touch. "I don't see a ring here," he said, pinching her ring finger between his thumb and pointer finger. He wiggled it teasingly and then dropped her hand back to the dock.

"Part of being good with relationships is knowing when to be in one and when not to be in one," she explained.

He raised a brow at her. "You don't think you should be in a relationship right now?"

She hated the direction of the conversation, but she feigned a shrug of indifference. Relationships did seem like a bad idea to her, at least right now. Until she could learn to control her bloodlust, she would end up murdering her lovers over and over again. While Geneva prided herself on her control of her emotions, she couldn't claim that she was unaffected by their deaths.

"It's not a matter of when," she continued, "but who. Why be in a relationship just to be in one? What's the point unless it gives you that heart-stuttering, soul-exploding feeling?"

Luke laughed again. "Soul-exploding?" he asked with a grin. He had to shout now to be heard over the increasing pounding of the rain.

"You know what I mean," she insisted. "Haven't you ever been in love?"

"Maybe," he replied. "How can you know for sure?"

She gave him a patronizing look. As the howling winds around them began to blow with more force, Luke had to strain to keep himself upright on the pier. Water from the ocean splashed around them as the waves mounted and crashed against the pier's legs.

Geneva was more than aware that it was getting too dangerous for him to be out here. As much as it would benefit her to send him away to the fishery so she can enjoy the storm without fretting over him, she wasn't quite ready to let go of his company. Besides, he would do her no good if his body was splayed lifelessly against the rocks below.

"Have *you* ever been in love, Geneva?" he shouted over the roar of the ocean.

Impatiently, Geneva lurched herself up to her feet and grabbed onto his hand. She ignored his question entirely as she heaved him up to a standing position, careful as to not slip on the wet dock. Luke was still grinning when he stood, his eyes amused and heated as he looked down at her with his impressive height. He was nearly a foot taller than her, a fact which seemed to put an endearing smile on his face.

"Come on," she urged. "Take me to the fishery."

The rain had plastered his hair around his head, yet, it only served to give him a charmingly boyish appearance coupled with the devious grin on his face. She wasn't sure what he was so delighted about, but she allowed him to take her hand in his and lead her down to the fishery.

He nearly slipped a few times on the slippery pier but managed to keep his balance as he pulled her in tow behind him. When they reach the door, they huddled beneath the tiny awning while he fiddled with his keys.

"Why do you have a key to the fishery?" she asked him, bracing her weight against his body to keep herself out of the torrent of rain.

He gave her a sly wink over his shoulder as he unlocked the door and pulled them both inside. "I'm close with the owner," he replied.

Luke panted and smoothed his drenched hair away from his face. His shirt was nearly translucent where it clung to his broad chest, at least, from what Geneva could see of it beneath those ridiculous fishing waders. Behind him was nothing but a dusty shack. The fishery was clearly in a state of disuse, though not entirely abandoned. There were fishing nets tangled and scattered all over the floor of the small space. Tall crates took up most of the room, leaving only a few feet for them to move around in.

She flicked the light switch by the door, casting a dim glow from the single bulb screwed into the ceiling above. The smell of fish was acrid in the air, tinted by the brine of the sea. Geneva wrinkled her nose as she glanced around the shack, looking for something to dry herself off with.

"It's not much, but it beats being out in the storm," Luke said.

Geneva ignored him. She spotted a thick wool blanket in the corner, a pair of fishing rods poking out from beneath it. She reached behind Luke, letting her body brush close to his as she yanked at the blanket. Dust filled the air around them, making Luke cough and splutter. She stepped away from him as she wrapped the blanket around her shoulders and dried herself off.

"Are you going to share?" he asked her with a raised brow.

She could see that he was shivering, goosebumps pebbled along his skin. She grinned with amusement and drew the blanket tighter around her body.

"I'm not that big on sharing," she said teasingly.

Luke took a step closer, putting them only a few inches away from one another. His eyes were low and heated on her as he reached for a corner of the blanket and tugged. She allowed him to yank it out of her grasp, to assert his manliness in this silly way to appease his ego.

He pulled the blanket until it was wrapped around both of their shoulders and drew their bodies even closer so they were pressed together.

His chest was solid and warm against hers, and she fought the urge to bury her face in his neck and inhale his masculine scent. She could already feel her fangs lengthening, her saliva flowing as she thought of the hot blood pulsing through him.

The rain was pounding against the roof as a low, grumbling thunder rattled the window. Luke rubbed her arms beneath the blanket, trying with futility to warm her.

"You're freezing," he murmured, resting his chin atop her head so he could tuck her against the warm contours of his body.

Geneva was trembling with restraint, which mercifully must have appeared to be shivering to him. She was so close to him she could feel the pulse in his neck against her forehead, and the beat of his heart against his chest.

In an act of defiance against her instinct, she wrapped her arms around his waist and held him close, refusing to pull away from him. If she looked into his eyes at that moment, she might be compelled to kiss him. If she kissed him, she wouldn't be able to stop herself from biting him, from draining the blood from his whole body. She was so hungry, and he smelled so *good*.

But she wasn't ready to kill him just yet. He wasn't ripe enough, and if she was being honest with herself, she was actually enjoying Luke's company.

"I want to see you again, Geneva," he said, his voice rumbling through his chest. "Can I take you out for coffee sometime? Someplace warmer and drier?"

Geneva melted in his arms, feeling an unusual softness in her soul. It had been a while since she went on an actual date rather than picking up someone at a bar. Romance had never been her cup of tea, but a nice quiet date with Luke sounded lovely. In fact, it would be the perfect way to sweeten his blood for her.

"Like a date?" she asked, pulling away to look at him, though she was terrified of what she would see.

It was worse than she imagined. His eyes were glimmering with heat and passion, lowered so that he was peering at her through his long, dark lashes. The pleasant flush under the scruff on his cheeks made him look young and innocent, like a bashful teenager asking a girl to prom.

"Yeah," he said blushingly, letting his gaze drift down to her mouth and settle there. "Like a date."

Geneva smiled at him and swallowed the lump forming in her throat. She was afraid to open her mouth for fear that he would see the sharp fangs hidden behind her lips. The urge to kiss him was overwhelming, but she knew how lethal it could be.

"Okay, Luke," she said, lowering her face back to his shoulder, which was somehow both more and less dangerous. "It's a date."

Chapter Three

Geneva drummed her fingers against her desk, staring at the coffee receipt in front of her. It was flipped upside down with Luke's number scribbled on the back in his mannish chicken scratch. Her eyes wandered across the thin paper, the stark blue numbers mocking her.

She had not given Luke *her* number, which put her in a delicate position. She liked it better when men made the moves, when they were the ones chasing her. To call him, felt like a violation of her code.

But there was no other option. If she wanted to see him again, she had to call him.

She sighed, glancing at the clock on the wall. She had no patients left for the day, but there was plenty of paperwork to be done and a few emails to be sent. She found it hard to pluck up the motivation to do any work. Her attention was constantly drawn back to the receipt, back to Luke's charming smile, and the rich, sweet scent of his blood.

In the back of her mind, she thought of Eugenia's dinner. Though she was reluctant to bring a date and comply with her sister's demand, she couldn't help but imagine what it would be like to bring Luke. He was a psychologist like her, and a handsome one at that. He was exactly the kind of man she envisioned herself lugging along to family events, wearing on her arm like an appeasing accessory.

Eventually, after the silent stillness of her empty office had become unbearable, Geneva picked up her phone and dialed the number on the receipt. Her stomach was fluttering while the dial tone buzzed in her ear.

"Hello?"

Geneva swallowed. "Hello," she said.

She hadn't thought of what she wanted to say, and now, she felt a sinking feeling in the pit of her stomach.

"Geneva?" asked Luke's voice on the other line. "Is that you?"

She nodded, but then remember that he couldn't see her. "Yes, it's me," she said, feeling heat bloom in her cheeks. She hated feeling so girlish and silly.

"It's good to hear from you, Geneva," he replied. She could hear the smile in his voice. "It's been a couple days. I didn't think I was going to hear from you ever again."

"A couple of days isn't that long," she teased. "You must have been waiting for my call."

He laughed, the sound causing static to crackle over the line.

"I'm *intrigued*," he corrected himself. "A mysterious woman on the pier could be a siren for all I know. A harpy. It's worth finding out, I think."

"A harpy?" she scoffed.

"Ah, don't play dumb," he said. "You're really a mythological creature hellbent on preying on men, aren't you?"

Geneva was glad that he wasn't in the room with her to see her startled impression. She may not be a siren, but a vampire was no better. Her intentions to prey on him suddenly felt silly and misplaced.

"I can only imagine you gave me your number so that you could be my next prey," she retorted. "Isn't that right?"

He laughed again, and she relished the sound, wanting to make him laugh more. Laughter sweetened the blood in such a light, refreshing way, like drinking happiness.

"Maybe so," he said. "Did you have any ideas?"

Geneva picked at her fingernails. The clock ticked menacingly on the wall, as if it was telling her to hurry it up and ask him out already.

"Grab a bite?" she suggested. "It's a little basic, but I thought it would be a nice, casual way for us to get to know each other a little bit more."

"I agree, babe," he said. "This afternoon? We can meet at that cute little burger joint downtown. You know, the one with the coffee corner that all the tourists go to?"

"Meat & Greet?" Geneva said with a chuckle. "Yeah, I can meet you there in a couple of hours. Sound good?"

"Sounds lovely," he replied. "See you soon."

Meat & Greet was crowded as usual when Geneva arrived that afternoon. She had gone home to change into a vibrant, red dress first, something casual but eye-catching. Something that looked like she just threw it on but screamed "I like you." With some red lipstick to match, she felt confident and powerful, the image of the vampire that she was, even if her fangs were hidden.

There was still a light afternoon drizzle darkening the foggy sky, so Geneva didn't have to be as careful to reapply copious sunscreen to avoid the burns night creatures like her were prone to. There was nothing less sexy than flesh melting off its bones.

She spotted Luke in the back of the line at the counter and moved to join him.

"Geneva," he said, wrapping his arms around her as she approached. "You look absolutely beautiful."

His hand came to the small of her back, and his head dropped down to plant a kiss on the top of her head. Geneva felt her body tingle under the domestic ministrations, a hot blush creeping up her neck all the way to her ears. She was not used to such casual affection.

"You look nice, too," she said, letting her gaze rove over his new state of dress.

Rather than fishing waders, he had opted to wear a dark suit, a charcoal grey blazer with a prim, white, collared shirt poking out from underneath. He was a completely different person, more alluring, somehow more mysterious.

"I think I clean up pretty good, don't you think?" he said, grinning down at her. "I imagine my fishing waders didn't exactly make a great first impression."

Geneva laughed. "I liked the fishing waders," she said. It wasn't really a lie. She may have been repulsed by them, but they were intriguing in their own way.

"Oh, Geneva, you're a terrible liar," he said. "Suits are more your speed. That's your type, isn't it? Stuffed shirts? Wealthy, powerful venture capitalists and hedge fund lawyers?"

She swatted him on the arm. "You think I'm a gold-digger?" she demanded. "I have a well-paying job. You know that."

"It's not about money, though, is it?" he asked, his tone light and teasing. "You like a powerful man, and why wouldn't you? A simple farmhand or pizza delivery boy definitely wouldn't be good enough for you."

Geneva crossed her arms over her chest, feeling attacked. "Well, I guess you got me all figured out now, don't you?"

Luke grinned at her again, giving her a sly wink. "I *am* a psychologist, babe," he reminded her. "And a damn good one, too."

Geneva rolled her eyes. "Well, so am I, Luke," she countered. "I think you may have a bit of an ego problem."

Luke burst into laughter as they stepped up to the counter. He ordered a number six combo with a small black coffee and stepped aside to let Geneva order a number four with a side of black tea with cream and sugar. After he paid for them both, and they collected their food, he led them to an empty table near the back of the restaurant.

"Am I wrong, Geneva?" he asked her, taking a bite into his juicy beef burger, cheese dripping down his fingers. "Tell me that powerful men aren't your type."

She took a swig of her tea and reached for another sugar packet to sweeten it even more. She couldn't help but notice that Luke drank his coffee black. It was hard for her to understand how he could drink the bitter stuff without something to sweeten it a little. Usually, she thought black coffee drinkers were pretentious, but she got the feeling that he actually just likes the bitterness.

"I don't have a type," she insisted.

"Nonsense."

"I don't!"

He gave her a skeptical look, fiddling with the handle on his mug. "If you don't have a type, then why are you interested in me?" he asked with one brow quirked in question.

"You're handsome?" she guessed. She had no idea what answer he was fishing for, though she would have loved to give it to him. Men were so pliable when they were given the things that they wanted.

"And?"

"And intelligent and charming," she continued. "Did you agree to come just so I would shower you with compliments?"

"I love to be showered with compliments," he replied. "It's so rare for us men. Please, keep them coming. Tell me how great I am."

Geneva laughed, not a fake one meant for seduction and manipulation, but a genuine girlish giggle.

"You were pretty great earlier today," she said because she did believe it.

But the longer she talked to him, the less it felt like he actually liked *her* rather than her attention. It was almost like tasting a dose of her own medicine. She wanted Luke to like her more, to obsess over her, and fall in love with her. Whatever this was, wasn't nearly good enough.

"What about me?" she asked, flipping the subject. "What do you like about me? Am I your type? What even is your type?"

Luke peered at her over the lip of his mug as he brought it up to his mouth for another sip. She watched him take a long swig, her gaze stuck on his sensual mouth.

"I like my women sweet," he said after a moment.

"Unlike your coffee."

He smiled. "Yes," he agreed. "I like a woman to be unbitter and unjaded. Sweet, affectionate, kind, empathetic. Someone caring and motivated to help others. Do you think that describes you, Geneva?"

No part of Geneva believed that his description applied to her. She was cold, bitter, and revolted by others. She felt no need to help people who couldn't help themselves, and the truth was that she was a bit disappointed in Luke for being so soft.

"Who could say that describes them without sounding arrogant?" she quipped.

"Are you calling me arrogant?" he teased.

She gave him a demure but scathing look from beneath her lashes, pursing her lips together. He was snarkier than she had given him credit for, and his antagonism was stirring the nerves in her body.

"You seem pretty conceited to me," she said flippantly.

"And you like that, don't you?" he pressed. "*That's your type.*"

Geneva rolled her eyes. "I don't have a type, Luke," she insisted. "I like men, plain and simple. My only trend is that I like *attractive* men."

Luke gave her a knowing look. "That's pretty subjective, don't you think?"

"No," she said with a shrug. "I think you are objectively handsome. Any woman in this room would say the same."

Luke looked around the room. There were plenty of women around, either serving burgers or chatting with their friends and families at the tables. The restaurant was noisy with clinking dishes and loud chatter.

As his eyes scanned the room, Geneva scanned him, searching his face for any clue about him. She knew now what his type was, and she could imagine the kinds of women in this room that he would go for – the shy cashier behind the counter, the girl in the corner at a table by herself with her nose buried in a book.

She was not that kind of sappy wallflower, but she knew how to play the part. She knew who she had to be to get Luke to fall in love with her.

"Luke?"

His gaze flicked back to her, eyes stormy and curious.

"Why did you decide to become a psychologist?" she asked.

He tapped his finger against his lips pensively.

"I'm curious about the human mind," he finally answered. "Part of me wanted to think I did it so I can help others, and I'll concede that it's a big part of it. But at the end of the day, I'm not all that altruistic. I think people are fascinating. I specialize in phobias, you know. People are afraid of the craziest, most innocuous stuff. The human brain is truly a mystifying piece of our puzzle, so different from the heart or the lungs. It can't be as predicted as easily, nor are there any simple cures for its ailments."

Geneva nodded emphatically, relieved to hear him put it so succinctly. "I agree completely," she said. "Sometimes, you think you've got the human mind mostly figured out, and then you meet someone who just shatters that perception. I like how unpredictable people are. I never know what kind of person is going to walk through my office door."

Luke's expression was warm and tender now. She picked up the sickeningly sweet cloy of his blood, and she knew it was pumping faster through his body when he looked at her.

"There is something magical about the office, isn't there?" he asked. "When you've got a patient in the chair, and it's just you and their brain."

He scratched awkwardly at the back of his neck, averting his gaze. His sudden shyness made Geneva cant her head to the side, curious.

"I have a tendency of… talking to women that way," he explained timidly, as if it was a horrible confession. "Like they were my patients. Picking their brains. You're a psychologist, too. Tell me I'm not the only one."

Geneva let out a laugh as she leaned closer. "It's hard not to sometimes," she said. "Especially when they don't even realize that you're doing it."

Luke sighed and picked through the remnants of his fries.

"I know it's certainly been the downfall of many of my relationships," he said, slamming his hand down on the table. "Is it presumptuous to think the experience had been the same for you?"

Geneva didn't want to lie to him, but she was afraid that she had to. The need to therapize her lovers only went so far as manipulating them. To pick their brains just for the hell of it would never happen for her, but it was true that it had been the downfall of her relationships. Just for an entirely different reason.

"How did it lead to their downfall?" she asked.

Luke gave an indifferent shrug. "Some of them feel like I'm trying to 'fix' them," he explained. "Others think I'm too analytical, and they feel like they're always being observed. I suppose I can understand that to some degree."

"You've had a lot of girlfriends, huh?"

He gave her a boyishly charming smile. "Are you jealous?"

"I can tell by your roguish smile that you're a ladies' man," she replied. "Even still, you've got the air of a gentleman."

"I don't kiss and tell, if that's what you're getting at."

They locked gazes over the table in a heatedly-amused glared. A smile tugged at Luke's lip, and unwittingly, Geneva's too.

"Finish your food, babe," he said. "It's getting cold."

After they left Meat & Greet, Geneva convinced Luke to walk her home. She didn't live far away, just a twenty-minute walk down the quaint, bustling downtown street. The small coastal town had its rustic charm, even if the pungent scent of salt water and cod lingered permanently in the air. Even from the city street, the smell of fish was acrid as they made their way down the sidewalk.

The glow of the streetlamps was just beginning to flicker on, casting warm but diluted light in tidy circles along the cobblestone.

"Where are you from?" Geneva asked Luke, wondering if he was born with the stink of fish on his skin, or if he came here on his own volition.

"Chicago," he replied casually.

She had to struggle to match his pace without running, but she still found herself toddling along beside him on the cobblestone path.

"What made you decide to move here?" she asked incredulously.

She had always felt like she belonged in a bigger city, somewhere with lots of people and lots of shadows. Her plans once her immortality became evident were to move to a place like New York or Los Angeles, somewhere she could blend in.

"The sea," he simply replied. "I love the sea. I love the small-town life. This place is way different from Chicago in pretty much every conceivable way. I don't have a lot of great memories there, and well, this place is just a refreshing change of pace."

Geneva glanced at him from the corner of her eye. "The sea?"

He nodded. "Yup!" he said. "I told you I like to fish, right? There's no place in the world like being on a boat out in the water, sandwiched between the sea and the sky. It's like being in space, Geneva. Indescribable."

"I remember," she said, recalling the void he had mentioned when they met on the pier.

He gave her a sidelong glance, a skeptical look on his face.

"You don't strike me very much as an outdoorsy person," he said. "What were you doing down at the pier that day? Call of the sea?"

Geneva shook her head.

"I just wanted to think," she explained. "I thought a change of scenery would be nice, and the fog was kind of creepy that day."

"You *liked* it?" he asked.

She shrugged. "It's not *that* morbid," she said defensively. "Lots of people prefer gloomy weather. It can't be sunny all the time."

Luke made a noise of disapproval with the back of his throat. "I wish it could be," he said. "I love the sun."

Geneva scoffed with disgust.

"Yeah, I can tell you don't, Snow White," he teased. "You've got skin like a wealthy Victorian woman. You'd probably get a sunburn just standing next to a window for five minutes."

Geneva glared at him.

"I *do* burn easily," she confessed. "The sun is an evil star, always killing us, giving us cancer and sunburns. To hell with the sun."

Luke laughed and clapped her on the shoulder. His palm was warm, and she had to resist the urge to press her mouth to the pulse she could feel hovering at his wrist.

"You're an interesting woman, Geneva."

"In a good way?"

Luke gave an indifferent shrug. Geneva scoffed at him indignantly. His resulting smile was enough to send more butterflies whirling through her stomach.

"I'm beginning to see why you have relationship trouble," she said wryly.

"Not *that* much trouble."

They came to the end of the neighborhood, where Geneva's house sat in the middle of the row. Luke followed her lead up the steps to the porch and leaned against the door frame of her front door.

"I had fun tonight, Geneva," he said, lowering his face so that he was in reach if she should decide she wanted to lean up and kiss him.

"So did I, Luke."

She thought of Eugenia's dinner again. Perhaps, it wouldn't be so bad to bring someone like Luke along, someone who would impress her sister. The thought of bringing some other stranger annoyed her. She knew she would struggle to find another man of Luke's caliber so quickly, and she didn't want to disappoint her sister anymore, at least, not when Luke was finally presenting himself for the job in such an enticing way.

"My sister is hosting a dinner party this weekend," she blurted, toying with the zipper on her purse. "It's just her, her husband, and one other couple. Would you like to be my date?"

Luke blinked at her, lifting his arm from where it was braced on the doorframe.

"Your sister?" he asked. "Isn't it a little soon to be meeting each other's family?"

Geneva recoiled as if she had been bitten.

"It's just a dinner party," she said. "It's casual, nothing fancy."

He hummed pensively. "I don't know," he said uncertainly. "Let's take things a little slow for now. Maybe we save meeting the family for something like a fifth date?"

Geneva frowned, casting her eyes down to her feet. It felt terrible to be rejected when he was standing so close to her, acting like he wanted to kiss her with his face impending so close to hers. She could tell that he would soon close the gap between them and press his lips against hers, but she was still crushed by his response to her invitation.

"So, will I get to see you again?" he asked, his voice low. He reached up to brush a lock of hair away from her face.

His blood was sweet in the air, but unappealingly so, like a scented candle or a rotting fruit. It was not yet ripe enough for drinking, and Geneva didn't quite have Luke where she wanted him. She *needed* him to come to that dinner.

And she had almost a week to make him.

"Sure, Luke," she said sweetly. "We'll see each other again."

Chapter Four

Now that Geneva knew Luke had her number, she felt less pressure to be the one to instigate things with him. Throughout work the next few days, she constantly checked her phone, waiting for his name to flash across the screen.

She didn't understand why he seemed so detached from her, like he was the one in control. When men often found her intimidating, it was hard to reckon with the fact that some didn't. Luke had displayed the full effect of his confidence. It wouldn't be as easy to impress him. In order to gain back some semblance of control, she had to find a way to get him to *want* to come to Eugenia's dinner.

The best way she could think to do that was by warming him up to her the old-fashioned way – seducing him, making him fall in love with her.

He had already given her a clue as to how. *Sweetness*. She was certain that word had never been used to describe her before, and the fact that it was something Luke looked for in a girl was only a slight set back. He didn't know what he really wanted, and when she shows him what he was missing out on, he would come around.

For now, she had to find a way to slip into the cracks, to gnaw at his brain the way he had gnawed at hers. Did he think about her constantly the way she thought about him? She wanted him so badly and wasn't quite sure where to start.

Her first order of business was to find him on social media. She wouldn't be able to do a good job of seducing him until she knew exactly who he was. She knew he was a psychologist specializing in phobias, a fisherman in his spare time, and liked sweet women. It was hardly enough to go on.

When she looked up his social media profiles, she found that he had a squeaky-clean reputation. He had a few pictures with his mother, and a couple of him at the beach with his friends. His status updates were benign things, congratulations to married couples, condolences for losses, a few political but relatively neutral posts.

She looked for any hints to past girlfriends in his profiles, but they had all been wiped clean of offending material. Either he never took any pictures with them, which seemed unlikely, or he wiped his social media clean of them when he was finished.

Geneva stumbled across a photograph of him at the bowling alley, wearing a ridiculously-looking bowling shirt and a cheesy grin. There was a woman standing beside him in the picture, dressed in tight jeans and a black blouse. She stood tall, her arm slung casually around his neck. A stab of hot jealousy ripped through Geneva's soul. If he had been so careful to remove everyone else, what was this woman still doing on his profile?

Curious, she scrolled down to the caption and found that it was his cousin, who was apparently a championship bowler. She could see that he had checked in there a number of times and attended bowling night pretty regularly.

She winced in disgust. The thought of putting her feet in a pair of shoes a sweaty stranger had worn was just as repulsive as the thought of sticking her fingers into a crusty bowling ball. She couldn't remember the last time she went bowling, but she supposed there wasn't any harm in showing up to the bowling alley.

According to the bowling alley's social media post, there was an event two nights from now. That was the day before Eugenia's dinner, so if Geneva played her cards right, she could find him there and convince him that he should come with her.

She already knew what she would wear – a "sweet" dress that her mother had given her a few years ago. The puffed sleeves and sweetheart neckline were not Geneva's style, but they would serve her purpose in this case. Fortunately for her, the dress was her favorite color, red. There was something romantic about the way the fabric flared out at the hips, and there was just a slight hint of cleavage at the neckline.

With her mind decided, she shut her laptop and got ready for bed. Though she wasn't eager to go to a bowling alley, she found herself excited to see Luke again.

***

A couple of days later, Geneva wore the sweet dress to work. She knew she would be going to the bowling alley that night, and she didn't want to go home and change before she headed there. She had her favorite perfume with her in her purse, and a tube of red lipstick to complete the look. She had even gone out and bought a pair of cute bowling shoes, unworn by another person, though she had them stashed beneath her desk until she was ready to leave.

At work, she received remarks on her dress, some positive, some just confused. Her older patients were quick to compliment her on the style, though it came with some backhands at the expense of her usual, clinical way of dressing.

She ignored their jabs, pretending that she felt confident in the dress despite how much she disliked the way it made her feminine frame look girlish and young.

Work was agonizingly slow, and when she finally headed out onto the street with her purse slung over her shoulder, she felt a wave of relief crash over her. She couldn't help but think about Luke all day, the scent of his blood, the allure of his dark eyes.

She had already changed into her bowling shoes, and as she walked the bustling street, she fished her lipstick out of her purse and used her compact mirror to apply it to her lips. A little mascara completed the look, and she felt ready to conquer the world by the time she walked into the bowling alley.

It was crowded inside, the place filled to the brim with middle-aged couples in kitschy bowling shirts and boisterous, drunken grins. It was a lively place for a Thursday night, the kind of crowd Geneva didn't often find herself in.

She scanned the faces in the crowd, looking for Luke amongst them. At first, she didn't think he even came. She felt a stab of disappointment low in her gut. Then she spotted the woman from the photograph, his supposed cousin.

The woman was grinning from ear to ear as she drew back the pink bowling ball in her hands. When she hit a strike, the crowd at her station all cheered loudly for her, a noise that was scarcely audible in the loud din of the room.

Geneva stepped closer, peering through the throngs of people, parting them so she could finally see Luke. She spotted him sitting at the table, a beer in one hand and the other draped over the empty chair beside him. He was cheering for his cousin, watching the score change on the screen above.

Nervously, Geneva glanced over at the bar. She would feel much better with a drink in her hand. At least, it might loosen some of the tension she felt in her chest.

At the bar, she ordered a light beer and took a few slow sips. To loosen the tightness in her chest, she took a seat at the bar and nursed her beer, taking a beat to assess the situation. She couldn't be too bold or clingy with him. She had to make their meeting seem accidental.

Her eyes quickly scanned the room, looking for a suitable distraction. She could easily make Luke come to her just by being herself. All she had to do was flit about the room like the social butterfly that she was. There were plenty of other men in here who could be useful to her.

At the lane adjacent to Luke's, she saw a tall man in a crisp white shirt, an expensive watch gleaming on his wrist. He looked rather out of place in the bowling alley, like he had just come from his high-rise corporate office to mingle with the commoners.

He's the perfect bait for Luke, Geneva thought.

She downed the rest of her beer and reapplied her lipstick. Her fingers skimmed through her dark hair in an attempt to tame it before she flipped it over her shoulder and made her way over to the man.

He was seated at the table, watching his peers bowl from the sidelines while he munched on a plate of nachos. His blue eyes flicked up to hers as she approached. They widened ever so slightly, and with a smug sense of satisfaction, Geneva saw him straighten his shoulders and sit up a little taller.

"Hi," she said, giving him a delicate flutter of her lashes.

"Hi," he echoed, shifting to the side so Geneva could slide into the booth beside him. She obligingly sat and flashed him with a coy smile.

"I saw you sitting by yourself from the bar," she explained. "It looked like you could use some company."

"Absolutely," he replied, returning her smile. "If it's not rude to say, you don't really seem like the bowling type."

Geneva quirked a brow at him. "I could say the same about you."

He shrugged and glanced over at his friends who were all crowded around the lane, cheering for someone's perfect three hundred.

"I'm just here to support my friends," he said. "Name's Caleb, by the way."

"Geneva," she replied, shaking his extended hand. "Honestly, it's not really my scene either. I was just looking for a little change of pace tonight."

She inched a little closer to him, inhaling the scent of pine and citrus cologne on his neck. Beneath his cheap drugstore scent was a sweet and tangy smell of blood. She couldn't help her devious grin as she decided that he would be her next meal. He would be a perfect appetizer for Luke's blood when it was finally ready.

"What do you do, Caleb?" she asked him, batting her lashes at him once more.

He gave her an arrogant smirk that she found highly amusing. His pearlescent teeth gleamed in the purple lighting above them as he leaned in a little closer to her.

"I'm a lawyer," he bragged.

"Oh? What type of law do you practice?"

Another flashy grin. "Criminal defense."

She scoffed at him and took another sip of her beer. She felt slightly less guilty about her plans to kill him later.

"And you?" he asked, unperturbed by her response.

"A psychologist," she replied.

He shifted even closer so that their thighs were pressed together. Her gaze was drawn to his mouth when he brought his beer up for another slow sip.

Beyond his head, Geneva saw Luke stand up from his seat and turn around. She knew immediately when he saw her. His whole body froze. With her attuned senses, Geneva could see the confusion on his face even from where she sat. It was there for only a second before it was replaced with a mischievous smile. She was surprised to see him wink at her before he walked over to the bar and sat down.

Geneva blinked. She crossed and uncrossed her legs, and then crossed her arms.

"Are you alright?"

She glanced back to Caleb's face to find his brow raised in question.

"I'm sorry," she said sweetly. "I'm just getting a bit of a headache."

He gave her a dubious look so she reached into her purse, fished out the wrapper of a chocolate bar, and wrote her number on the back.

"I hope you'll call me," she said, pressing it into his hands.

Caleb looked at the wrapper and carefully folded it before putting it into his wallet. His eyes started a roving glance from her lap up to her eyes, lingering a little longer in places that they shouldn't. He locked gazes with her when she cleared her throat.

"Will do, Geneva," he said with a smirk. "I hope you feel better."

She murmured her gratitude and slipped out of the booth. Luke was still seated at the bar, his back against the counter so he could watch his cousin bowl. Geneva approached him, curious to see if he was jealous.

"Luke," she purred, stopping in front of him as she passed the bar. "How funny to run into you here. Fishing *and* bowling, huh?"

He narrowed his eyes at her, a teasing smile playing at his lips.

"How funny," he repeated. "I would never have thought I'd catch you in a place like this. Tell me, Geneva, what brings you to the bowling alley?"

Geneva was annoyed by his suspicious tone. She set her empty beer bottle down on the counter with a heavy clunk and crossed her arms over her chest.

"Looked like you were on a date," he ventured.

There was something smug about the way he watched her, like he had caught her in the act and was highly entertained.

She shook her head at him. He didn't seem jealous to have seen her pressed up against another man, and she wasn't sure that was the right tactic anymore.

"Not a date," she explained. "I was just looking for someone to bring to my sister's dinner this weekend."

Luke rolled his eyes at her.

"I promised her I would bring a date," she lied. "I wanted it to be someone impressive, but it's getting to be crunch time. Any average guy will have to do."

He gave her a disapproving look. "Did you ask that guy?"

"What guy?"

His eyes narrowed at her even further, if that were even possible. He pointed over her shoulder at the table where Caleb was still sitting.

"That guy who's been staring at you since you walked over here."

"Oh, him?" she asked dismissively. "No. Not impressive enough."

"Really, Geneva?" Luke chided. "Tell me you aren't that classist."

"He's a criminal defense lawyer."

"My mistake," he said apologetically. "Surely, there's someone else in this bowling alley who is impressive enough to bring to your sister's dinner."

"I'm sure there is," she agreed, letting her gaze wander over him at her leisure. Regardless of how silly it looked, the tacky shirt fit him well, hugging his well-defined muscles.

"Take your pick," he said. "I'll be your wingman."

Now, it was her turn to give him a disapproving look.

"Luke, I don't need a wingman," she said. "You pick. I'm sure you're a better judge of character than I am. Who's the most impressive man in this room?"

He opened his mouth and then closed it again. His eyes darted around the slim pickings in the room. They lingered on Caleb, who had still yet to take his from Geneva's back. She wondered if he'll still call her later after seeing her flirt at the bar when she said she had a headache.

"After deliberation, I've found that the most impressive man in here is me," he said.

Geneva stared at him.

"I suppose this means I have the responsibility to take you to your sister's dinner," he said with defeat. "I can't allow you to go with anyone subpar, certainly not a criminal defense lawyer."

She blinked at him and uncrossed her arms. "Are you serious?"

"Yes, babe. What time should I pick you up?"

She was skeptical of his acquiescence, but she didn't press it since this was what she had wanted anyway. He was still wearing that smug expression, and she could tell by the scent of his blood that he was no sweeter, no more ready for her to taste. She wasn't quite sure what to make of him. It was hard to pinpoint what he wanted from her.

"Seven thirty?" he asked when she said nothing.

Geneva nodded.

"See you then, babe."

Chapter Five

That weekend, when Geneva knocked at Eugenia's door with Luke standing at her side, she felt an overwhelming apprehension. There was something bitter about the scent of his blood today, and she wondered if it may have been a mistake to bring him.

He was dressed sharply, nothing silly about his simple shirt and trousers. They were tailored well to his body, and he seemed very aware of how good he looked. He snuck furtive glances at Geneva like they were a slow acting poison, and she would eventually succumb to him.

She had every intention of flipping that notion on its head. She was actually beginning to grow fond of Luke, even if she was a little frustrated by his aloofness.

Eugenia swung the front door open, beaming from ear to ear. Her eyes drank in the man standing next to her sister, and she glanced at Geneva with a tacit look of approval.

"Welcome," she said, stepping back so they could enter the house. "I'm Eugenia, Geneva's sister," she said extending her hand to Luke. "It's nice to meet you."

Luke shook her hand, returning her smile.

"Nice to meet you as well," he replied. "I'm Luke."

Eugenia led them into the dining room where the table was set with fancy dinner plates and glasses of white wine. Seated at the table were four people, two of whom Geneva recognized as Eugenia's colleagues. The other two, complete strangers to her. Eugenia introduced everyone to each other as Geneva and Luke took their seats.

One of the couples was comprised of two of Eugenia's colleagues from work. The woman was a voluptuous blonde with clear honey eyes, Melanie, and her husband, a demure and mousy-looking man with dark glasses and curly hair named Mark.

The other couple was a prim set of dark brunettes, the man as pale as Geneva, and the woman deep and lovely. According to Eugenia, their names were Hunter and Bambi, which at first, Geneva thought was a joke, but no one else seemed to be laughing so she didn't. That was Parker's sister and brother-in-law, which meant that Eugenia, for some reason, thought Geneva could ever been friends with a woman named Bambi.

As the table filled with polite chatter, Eugenia went into the kitchen and returned with a platter of grilled salmon and asparagus. She was all smiles and dimples as she passed it around the table, urging everyone to delight in her secret recipe.

"So, Luke," she said as she took her place beside her husband, Parker, at the table. "What do you do for a living? Forgive me, but Geneva hasn't mentioned anything about you before."

Luke smiled politely at her. "I'm a psychologist," he replied. "Just like Geneva. Isn't that something?"

"That *is* something," Eugenia said, giving Geneva a strange look. "Was that how you two met? At work?"

Luke shook his head. "We met on the pier, actually," he explained. "Can you believe that she was sitting out there earlier this week during the middle of that thunderstorm? I saved her life that day."

"You did *not* save my life," Geneva objected. "I was perfectly fine out there without you disturbing my peace."

Luke gave her a teasing smile and nudged her with his elbow. "Play along, babe, I'm trying to impress your sister."

Geneva gave him a scathing look, but she found his antics charming and amusing. The frustrating part was that even though she'd convinced him to come to the dinner, it still felt like *he* was the one in control.

As everyone around the table dug into their salmon, and the couple across from Geneva devolved into a political argument with Parker, Luke started reaching for Geneva's leg beneath the lace tablecloth.

At first, the touches were fairly innocent – a light pat on the knee or a sweeping brush against her as he reached for her hand. The scent of his blood turned sweeter by the second, tinged with the flavor of his desire for her. It cloyed the air so strongly that she wondered how humans could be so blind to the smell.

The argument on the other side of the table grew more intense. Parker was beginning to get visibly frustrated, stammering out his sentences through his blustering red cheeks. Eventually, he had enough of whatever the pale man named Hunter was saying and slammed his fist down on the table.

"Parker," Eugenia said soothingly, reaching for his arm. "Just calm down, Parker."

Her husband looked at her, and almost instantaneously, his anger melted. Geneva had always been amazed by the relationship between Eugenia and Parker, how they worked so well at calming each other down, and how they never seemed to get one another riled up.

"Perhaps, we should talk about something else," Luke suggested. "Did anyone here know that Geneva likes to bowl? Maybe I don't know her that well, but doesn't that seem out of character for her?"

A strange tension filled the room as every eye turned to look first at Luke and then at Geneva, who twisted her fingers together nervously under the table. She now sorely regretted her choice to bring Luke, or even come at all.

"I like bowling," said Bambi. "I'm not very athletic, but at least I can pretend I am with bowling. I'm actually pretty good."

Luke cocked his head to the side. "Are you?" he asked. "I'm not bad either. I know it's kind of lame, but I like bowling, too. It made for a pretty good date night. Right, Geneva?"

Geneva chanced a look at her sister to find her grinning arrogantly at her. They both knew Luke was right – she was not a bowler. In fact, she was still disgusted when she remembered being there at the bowling alley under the dim purple light, surrounded by sweaty people lugging around bacteria-ridden bowling balls.

"I think I preferred being stuck in that fishing hut," Geneva said snidely.

Luke scoffed. "The fishery isn't a *hut*," he insisted.

"Oh, you like fishing, too?" Bambi asked. "My father used to fish every weekend. He'd let me tag along once I was old enough. There's nothing like being out on the water, is there?"

Luke smiled at her. Geneva felt a burning hot stab of jealousy in her chest. She didn't know who this Bambi woman thought she was, but if she thought she had a chance with Luke, she would have to get through Geneva first.

"Is that why you reek of fish?" Geneva snapped.

"Geneva!" Eugenia shrieked.

"That's probably the salmon you're smelling, babe," Luke said, glancing at her with amusement. She could see that it was at her expense and felt her cheeks warm up.

Luke's blood was incredibly enticing now. She couldn't help but notice how he got excited by her fluster and flush, his eyes darker and more heated when they roved over her. It drove the hunger brewing in her bones, her thirst for blood. She knew she wouldn't be able to control herself with Luke enough to take just a taste of his blood, so she hoped Caleb would call her soon so she could quench her thirst.

Eugenia was flustered by the disastrous direction of her dinner party and pulled her napkin out of her lap to lay it gently on the table.

"Geneva, could you help me with dessert in the kitchen?" she asked.

Geneva nodded and scooted her chair back from the table, happy for a chance to get out of the stifling air in the dining room. Luke reached for her hand as she stood up and gave it a light squeeze, then kissed the back of it and winked at her.

Feeling a tingling in her spine, Geneva carefully extracted her hand from his grasp, giving him a dry look, and followed her sister into the kitchen. She had prepared little glasses filled with layered banana pudding and pulled them from the fridge.

When she set them on the counter with a loud clatter, she put her hands on her hips and fixed Geneva with a stern glare.

"What's the matter with you?" she demanded. "Are you trying to ruin my party?"

"No, of course not," Geneva said defensively. "It's that brat, Bambi."

"She's not being a brat," Eugenia yelled. "You're acting jealous over nothing. Luke, whoever he is, has you *that* wrapped around his finger? According to him, you guys only met this week at the pier. What the hell?"

"I am *not* wrapped around his finger," she insisted.

Eugenia quirked a disbelieving look at her.

"I'm not buying it," she said. "I know how you get with men."

Geneva crossed her arms over her chest and let out an indignant scoff. "Oh, really?" she retorted. "How do I get with men?"

"Oh, come on, Geneva," Eugenia said, passing her a box of vanilla wafers to garnish the cups of banana pudding with.

Geneva snatched the box out of her hand and ripped it open.

"I want to know," Geneva said sneeringly. "Since you seem so certain that you know so much about me. Please, enlighten me."

"It's not like that, Geneva," Eugenia said patiently. "You know how you get. You get so obsessed and jealous all the time. Don't you think it's a little much? I can already see it happening with Luke, only, I can tell he's not going to be the kind of guy to roll over and put up with your nonsense."

"I'm not obsessed *or* jealous," she replied.

"If you're not jealous, then why do you think she's a brat?"

"Fishing *and* bowling?" Geneva demanded. "Who likes that stuff? She's openly flirting with him. And in front of her husband, too!"

"Geneva, it's not a crime to like fishing and bowling," Eugenia said with a sigh. "Obviously, Luke likes them."

"That's different."

Eugenia quirked a brow at her.

"I know I put a lot of pressure on you to bring a date, but you didn't have to," she said, her voice filled with regret. "I'm sorry for doing that. I get the feeling that you like Luke, and maybe bringing him here for this was a little rash."

Geneva let out a bitter chuckle.

"So, *do* you like him?" Eugenia pressed. "You didn't just snag him up for this dinner party, did you?"

Geneva nodded. "Yes, I like him," she conceded. "At least, I like him more than I've liked most other men. I don't know… He's just very compelling."

Sometimes, Geneva wanted to confess her vampirism to Eugenia, but she knew her sister already thought of her as a monster in other ways. She had always been the colder and more calculating one of the two of them. To add being a vampire on top of that would just take it over the edge. Geneva didn't *want* to be this way, but it was just how her mind worked.

"Compelling?" Eugenia asked. "Well, he's certainly handsome, I'll give you that. And how interesting that he's a psychologist. I think that might be good for you. You need to be the one in the hot seat every once in a while. Just to know what it feels like."

"What hot seat?" Geneva asked.

"You know, *the* hot seat," Eugenia insisted. "You go all 'therapist' on people, put them in the hot seat, make them answer all your questions."

Geneva popped a vanilla wafer into her mouth and gave Eugenia a pointed look. "I know how to separate my job from my personal life," she said firmly.

Eugenia gave a skeptical shrug. "I'm not so sure about that, Geneva," she said. "You tend to analyze people a lot. I can't imagine it's easy being your boyfriend."

"Hey!"

"Come on, let's get back in there," Eugenia said. "I don't want to keep my guests waiting."

For the rest of dinner, Geneva tried to stay on her best behavior. She ignored all conversation unless someone specifically addressed her, in which case, she gave a curt but polite reply.

Eugenia seemed proud of her for her restraint, and how she didn't try and force herself into conversations, particularly when Bambi voiced her opinion on something. It did, unfortunately to Geneva, seem like she was flirting with Luke. She wasn't blind to the sly glances she snuck at him when she thought no one was looking.

Geneva couldn't exactly blame her for looking, but her nerves were raised any time she spoke to Luke, or Luke spoke to her.

Luke, much to Geneva's dismay, ate up her discomfort. She believed he might be a sadist from how much enjoyment he seemed to be getting from her suffering. The only silver lining in the situation was that Luke's attention and focus were still on *her*, rather than Bambi, who was only a tool for his amusement.

After dinner, Luke offered to walk Geneva home. She accepted, and after she had said her goodbyes to everyone, she looped her arm around his, and they took to the streets.

She was a little buzzed from the wine, her belly full from the delicious meal her sister had made. Despite the less-than-ideal way the dinner party had gone, Geneva still felt satisfied and content. Luke was warm against her side, his blood sweet and pumping quickly.

"I learned something about you tonight," Luke said teasingly, reaching up to ruffle her hair as if she was a child.

Playfully, she swatted his hand away.

"What did you learn?" she asked.

"You are a jealous, jealous woman," he laughed.

Geneva growled in frustration, feeling attacked from all angles. She supposed it should be a moment of introspection for her. She *was* jealous, even if she didn't want to admit it. And perhaps, Eugenia was right. Maybe she *did* get a little obsessed. But Luke was different. Or at least, he could be.

"Okay, fine, maybe I'm a little jealous," she confessed. "I can't control it. Is it really that bad?"

Luke gave an indifferent shrug. "I kind of like it, actually, Geneva," he said. "You've got a quality about you that makes things like that seem kind of cute."

"What quality?" she pressed.

He reached for her hand as they walked and twined their fingers together. She gazed up at his profile, waiting for him to speak. He took a moment to think, tapping his finger against his lips pensively.

"Well, you're so confident in yourself that the jealousy didn't seem like something that came from lack of self-esteem," he explained. "I think it came from a possessiveness. I think you're the kind of person who's territorial with her things. Am I right?"

Geneva gave him a scathing look.

"Well, I guess you've got me pegged," she said bitterly.

Luke laughed at her and brought her hand up to his mouth to kiss the back of it. The sensation sent butterflies fluttering up through her stomach.

"No, I like it," he said with a grin. "Most women, knowing my profession, tend to be pretty guarded around me, careful about showing things like that. It's refreshing to see, honestly."

"What about you?" she asked, flipping the table. She was tired of all the conversations today being about her. "You saw me with that guy at the bowling alley, and you didn't seem jealous at all."

"Do you want me to be jealous?" he asked, his smile both smug and sweet.

Geneva let out a groan of frustration and threw her arms into the air.

"Do you always have to be so difficult?" she asked accusingly.

"I *was* a little jealous, Geneva," he conceded. "That guy was pretty attractive. But I couldn't be jealous of him, of anyone, unless you were mine. No one can steal you away from me if I don't have you yet."

"Yet?" she teased. "What's your end game with me, Luke?"

He shrugged noncommittally and threw his arm around her shoulder so he could pull her close against his side.

"Well, I don't know, Geneva," he said. "I've been thinking about kissing you all night. Should we start there?"

They came to an empty street corner and stood at the crosswalk. Luke grabbed her by the shoulders and turned her to face him. Geneva allowed him to move her, enthralled by how sure and strong his hands seemed on her body. One hand came up to cup her cheek, and he leaned down to press a searing kiss on her mouth.

She sank into his embrace, her fingers twisting in the fabric of his shirt. The streetlight's glow gilded his skin, making him look older, more refined. The scent of his pumping blood was thick in the air, and she could feel her fangs starting to lengthen in her mouth, pressing against her tongue.

Carefully, she kissed him back with as much fervor as she trusted herself with. She knew she couldn't deepen the kiss too much and risk accidentally biting him. She knew that as soon as she drew blood, Luke would be dead.

She inhaled the scent of him, savoring him. She wanted to poke her tongue out and taste his skin, but she forced herself not to.

"Geneva," he said softly when he pulled away from her. There was a dazed smile on his lips, and a glazed look in his eyes.

"Luke," she replied, running her palm up his arm to his muscular shoulder.

"Despite what a fool you made of yourself tonight, I had a really good time with you," he said through a cheesy grin.

"I can't tell if you're teasing me or not," she said.

"Well, you're smart enough to figure it out."

She gave him a stern look, but in a moment of tenderness, she reached up and pushed a dark curl away from his forehead. Luke leaned away from her touch, taking her wrist in his hand and pulling it back down to her side.

"You're so confusing, Luke," she said.

"I thought you were a psychologist."

She swatted him on the arm and glared at him.

"Are you going to call me, Luke?" she asked as they came to the front porch of her house.

She took the few steps up to the door and turned back to face him. He stood at the bottom of the stairs, putting them at eye level with each other.

"Maybe," he said, scooting just a little closer so he could kiss her one more time.

Geneva sighed into his mouth, half from frustration, half from pleasure.

"Goodnight, Geneva."

"Goodnight, Luke."

Chapter Six

Geneva worked herself into a frenzied lather in the days following Eugenia's dinner. She was embarrassed about her behavior that night, or at least, ashamed that Eugenia had called her out on it. Despite the horror she felt at the memory of it, she still couldn't get Luke out of her mind. He was not sweetening to her the way she wanted him to. It was starting to cast doubts in her mind about whether she was going about it the right way.

He remained standoffish and aloof, ignoring the few texts she had sent to him in the days following their somewhat awkward date.

She wanted to ask him on another date, but it was discouraging that he didn't seem to be all that interested in her. She adamantly followed him on his social media profiles, watching to see if another woman popped up anywhere in any of his pictures. She could think of no other explanation as to why he was so cold and distant toward her. There must be some reason why he hadn't fallen prey to her affections yet.

Since his attention seemed fickle and slippery, Geneva decided to take a step back and reassess the situation. Chasing after him obsessively could drive him further away, so Geneva tried to push him out of her mind for a while before she made her next move.

After work one day, rather than heading home to stew in her frustration, Geneva went to the coffee corner at Meat & Greet to sip some black tea and eavesdrop on potential future victims. Caleb, from the bowling alley, still hadn't called her yet, but she expected to hear from him soon. Unlike Luke, his blood had been primed for her already.

Until then, she needed someone to tide her over.

At the coffee corner, she headed to the counter where a short, dark-haired man waited to take her order.

She could tell by the scent of his blood that he found her attractive. Even if it weren't for the sickly-sweet smell in the air, she could see it in the red flush on his cheeks, and the shy way he avoided making direct eye contact with her.

"Black tea, two sugars, one cream?" he asked as she pulled out her wallet.

She blinked at him.

"How did you know?"

"You come here often," he replied. "I've seen you before."

Geneva stared at him as she swiped her credit card.

"And you remembered my order?" she asked suspiciously.

He gave her a shy smile, a pleasant one that Geneva found adorable. His eyes wandered her face, and then skimmed a little lower before he blushed again and busied himself preparing her tea. When he handed the steaming paper cup over to her, Geneva caught his gaze and tilted her head at him.

"You saw me here with that guy the other day?" she asked. "That tall, handsome one?"

He nodded at her. Her eyes flick to the nametag on his chest, affixed to the dark brown apron he wore. *Michael* was the name gleaming back at her in gilded letters.

"Well, Michael, do you think he and I make a cute couple?"

He blinked at her, his hand flying to the nametag. He ran his fingers over it hesitantly, then a slow smile came across his face.

"I think so," he replied. "I think any couple you're a part of would be cute."

Geneva smiled at him and took the cup from his hands.

"I'm glad you agree," she said. "I just wish I could get *him* to agree."

Michael frowned at her and rubbed his palms on his apron. Geneva, feeling generous, fished a ten-dollar bill out of her wallet and shoved it into the tip jar. She thanked Michael and found a place to sit down in the corner where she had a good view of everyone.

There weren't too many people inside at this time of day. It was nearing sundown, and coffee wasn't on everyone's mind so much anymore. There were a few stragglers sitting at the tables near the window, watching the sunset over the street.

Geneva sipped at her tea, watching the people by the window as they devolved into a fit of laughter over something one of them whispered into the other's ear. Her gaze was drawn back to Michael, who was cleaning the espresso machine behind the counter.

She watched him for a moment, fascinated by the intricacies of the mundane task. His hands were careful and sure as they swept across the machine with the cloth. For a second, she wondered what his hands would feel like on her body.

He might be a better snack for her than Caleb. She contemplated whether she should have a taste of him tonight when her phone began to vibrate in her purse.

When she fished it out, she didn't recognize the number that flashed across the screen. She answered it in a brusque, curt tone.

"This is Geneva."

"Good evening, Geneva," said a silky voice on the other line.

"Caleb," she purred. "I was just thinking about you."

"Were you?" he asked teasingly. "I was thinking about you, too. I was wondering if you were free tomorrow night. I want to take you to dinner. Some place that doesn't have neon lights or sweaty shoes."

Geneva laughed. Her gaze was still drawn toward Michael, who made eye contact with her over the counter before he quickly looked away. Now, she had a choice. She could wait until tomorrow and feed on Caleb, or take Michael home with her tonight. Either way would be easy, would be a distraction from Luke, at least for a little while.

She decided that Caleb would make a finer snack for her this time. He was attractive and interested in her, and since she already had him on the line, she might as well.

"What did you have in mind?" she asked Caleb.

"Carmello's?" he asked.

It had been a while since she'd been to the upscale Italian restaurant on the popular downtown corner where any tourism the small town got tended to flock. It was exactly the kind of place she liked for men to take her, so she was excited to hear his suggestion.

"That sounds lovely," she agreed. "Pick me up tomorrow night?"

"Yes, ma'am," he said. She could hear the grin in his voice.

When she hung up, Michael caught her eye again. She watched him dry his hands on a towel and then walk over to a table near hers to wipe it down.

"Was that your guy?" he asked her good-naturedly.

She didn't detect jealousy, though she assumed he must have felt it. He seemed rather interested to know, and she couldn't think of another reason.

"No, it wasn't," she said wistfully. "I'm not sure he likes me all that much."

"That's nonsense," he said. "Who wouldn't like you?"

She gave him a docile, demure grin, though she was well aware of her effect on men. It irked her to no end that Michael and Caleb seem so susceptible, yet, Luke seemed to be slipping through her fingers.

"I don't know," she said with a shrug. "I do my best to be likeable and charming."

Michael flashed her a grin that made her insides feel like jelly.

"You've succeeded," he said. "Maybe likeable and charming just aren't his type. Some guys just aren't into the right girls."

Geneva laughed embarrassingly at that. Michael had a kind, patient voice, and something about his face was unguarded and vulnerable. As a psychologist, she found that to be a dangerous quality in a person, a quality she tried to emulate for her patients. It made them want to confess things to her, and she could already feel herself wanting to confess things to Michael.

"I'm not sure I *am* the right girl," she said. "I'm not that special."

Michael scoffed at her. "You don't think as highly of yourself as I do," he replied. "You're a catch. I wish you could see that."

Geneva gave him a patronizing smile. "You're a barista, Michael," she said patiently. "What would you know about it?"

Michael was visibly stung. He withdrew his towel from the table he was wiping and tucked it into his back packet. His cheeks were flushed when he turned to look at her and gave her a disappointed frown.

"I don't know what that's supposed to mean," he said softly. The look of pain on his face was almost unbearable, even for Geneva.

"I'm sorry, Michael," she said sincerely. "I didn't mean it like that. It's just that to you, everyone must seem like a catch."

Michael let out an indignant scoff and turned his heel on her.

"Michael," she called after him.

He went behind the counter. She watched him, feeling guilty. He took a few orders while Geneva continued watching, unable to focus on anything else. She didn't usually feel shame or guilt where the feelings of strangers were concerned, but Michael was just trying to be nice. She felt something gnawing at her, urging her to apologize to him again, to make things right.

After he had tended to a few customers, he returned to her table with another hot cup in his hands. He set it down in front of her and gave her a pointed look.

"This is coffee," he said. "I figured you could use a pick-me-up. You seem kind of cranky."

Geneva was too startled to be offended.

"I'd rather have a banana nut muffin," she teased.

"You're pushing it, ma'am."

She gave him a bashful smile and batted her lashes at him.

"You can call me Geneva," she told him. "I'm really sorry for what I said. I didn't mean to offend you. Sometimes, I don't have much of a filter."

"Well, at least you're honest, Geneva," he said.

A brief beat of silence passed between them. He tilted the corner of his mouth in a grin, and she realized how young he seemed. He couldn't be more than a year or two younger than her, but something about his demeanor was child-like and innocent. It wasn't exactly a bad thing, Geneva thought. In fact, she found it kind of refreshing.

"Michael, do you think I can ask you for some advice?" she asked him.

"Are you sure you want advice from a lowly barista?" he asked.

Geneva chuckled nervously. "Yes," she said emphatically. "Any man will do. I just want to know what I should do about Luke. I'm worried I'm pushing him further away."

Michael sat down on the chair across from her and steepled his hands on the table.

"Men aren't all the same," he explained. "I need to know a bit more about him. All I know is that he seems pretty full of himself, from what I saw."

"Well, he's a psychologist, like me," she told him. "He likes fishing and bowling, and he's got kind of an aloof attitude."

Michael laughed. "He doesn't really sound like your type."

Geneva rolled her eyes.

"How do you know what my type is?"

"Well, you don't strike me as the fishing type," he said. "Do you think you'd ever go fishing with him? Maybe try taking an interest in his hobbies."

Geneva wrinkled her nose in disgust.

"See," Michael snickered. "You don't even want to go fishing with him. You probably also don't want to go bowling with him. Why do you even like this guy?

"He's intriguing," she said defensively. "There's a lot to like about him. For one, we have the same job, so we have lots in common. Two, he's really good-looking. Three, he's got this charisma that—"

"Alright, enough," Michael said, holding his hands up in defeat. "I get it. He's the whole package. Maybe he's just the kind of guy who likes to take things slow."

Geneva shook her head. "I don't think so," she said.

"You think he's just playing hard to get?" he suggested.

This was the first theory Geneva had heard that she actually liked. Perhaps, Luke *was* just playing hard to get. That *did* make the game a little more fun sometimes, though Geneva would prefer if *she* was the one who was hard to get.

"Maybe," she ventured. "If that's his game, what do you think I should do?"

Michael shrugged. He rested his chin on his hand and gave her a curious look. There was something faintly salty in the air, a scent that Geneva had a hard time identifying. For a moment, she thought it was blood, and her fangs started to prod at her gums.

Then she noticed the pulse in Michael's neck beneath the pale skin on the column of his throat. Her breath quickened as her stomach growled loudly.

"Do you want that banana nut muffin?" he asked, quirking a brow at the gurgling of her stomach. He seemed faintly intrigued, not realizing what danger he was in. She couldn't take her eyes away from the pumping vein in his neck, so she nodded, hoping that he would walk away and give her some respite.

When he got up, the salty, faintly sweet smell of his blood faded. She took a deep breath, staring down onto her lap until she felt her fangs recede back into her gums. She had to be careful about letting herself get too hungry for blood. It had been a while since she had attacked someone carelessly. She wasn't eager to fall back into that habit.

So, when Michael returned with that banana nut muffin on a small saucer for her, Geneva ate it quickly, trying not to focus on the way Michael was watching her, how that fact seemed to make his blood that much more tempting.

"Thanks for the advice," she said to him. "And for the coffee and the muffin."

Michael smiled at her. He didn't sit down this time. The place was starting to fill up with late night patrons, and a line had started to form at the cash register.

"You're welcome, Geneva," he said sincerely. "I hope I'll see you around."

"Sure," Geneva replied. "Me, too."

***

The next day, Geneva prepared all day for her date with Caleb. For a meal, she had to create just the right scenario for her to feasibly get away with attacking someone. If she drank too much of his blood and killed him, she might draw attention to herself. If she didn't drink enough, he would remember what she had done. It was even possible that he might become a vampire himself if she didn't drink just the right amount.

She also wanted to avoid drawing attention to herself, so her goal for the night was to get him to take her to his home. It would be secluded and private there, and she could feed without worrying that someone might catch her. Then she could easily slip away while he was still punch drunk on the feel of her fangs, or better yet, she could kill him.

The sleek black dress she chose to wear was tight, but comfortable, an outfit that hugged her curves just right. Paired with her favorite black lipstick, she was ready to break hearts by the time she stepped out onto the street.

During the night, when the sun was down, she didn't have to be as careful. Her power coursed through her a little more strongly, and her senses were slightly more attuned than usual. She sniffed the brisk air and caught a whiff of something familiar.

Caleb was waiting for her in a parked black sedan just in front of her house. She approached the passenger window and knocked.

He rolled down the dark tinted windows, his face a mixture of delight and bewilderment.

"How did you know which car was mine?" he asked.

"I'm smarter than you give me credit for," she teased as she slid into the seat beside him.

He was wearing more of that cheap cologne, but it paled in comparison to the strong scent of his blood. Her fangs came out once more, so Geneva gave him a tight-lipped smile.

She sensed his arousal as they drove to the restaurant. It wasn't far from where she lived, so in a matter of minutes, they were turning the corner of the street and pulling into the parking garage. Geneva reached for his hand and twined their fingers together, edging her body up closer to his. The scent of his blood was pungent and thrumming, so sweet she worried she wouldn't be able to make it through dinner.

But the thought of consuming her meal in the bathroom or in the backseat of his car disgusted her. She wanted to take her time, to really feed and enjoy this so she didn't have to worry about her impulses so much with Luke.

"Carmello's is a bit more your speed than the bowling alley, I'm assuming," Caleb said, holding the door into the restaurant open for her. "You look absolutely gorgeous tonight."

Geneva flicked her gaze to him and then demurely looked away. She pulled her hair away from her shoulder so the nape of her neck was exposed. The scent of her musky vanilla perfume wafted through the air between them.

"Thank you," she replied, her voice soft and silky smooth. She felt good tonight.

When they sat down at their table, she imagined that it was Luke across from her instead of Caleb. She thought of his dimpled smile and broad shoulders. She imagined the silly things he might have to say about fishing, or the amused chuckled he always seemed to be letting out at her expense.

Caleb didn't have much to say, and Geneva wasn't keen on conversation with him anyway. Instead, she focused on the taste of her food, on how delicious she imagined Caleb's blood tasting. Occasionally, she brushed her foot against Caleb's calf beneath the table and caught his eye with a sly grin.

The more she flaunted herself, the sweeter his blood tasted in the air. The coppery tang was almost unbearable as the dinner date dragged on. When the waitress brought out a dessert menu, Geneva politely declined. The eagerness that flashed across Caleb's face was reassuring, though just by the scent of him, she didn't need it.

He invited her back to his place and drove her through the upscale parts of town to the secluded, gated neighborhood where he lived. His house was too massive for one person to live in, though he assured her that he lived alone. She wondered how Luke lived, if he was the type to flaunt his wealth like this.

As Caleb led her into the house, Geneva looped her arm around his and hovered close to him, pressing her body against his side. That got his blood pumping faster, and soon, she wouldn't have to reign in her thirst any longer.

"You know, most women just want me for my money," he said with gusto. "It's nice to meet someone who wants me for my body."

Geneva let out a rich chuckle and slid even closer to him. Her hands came to the back of his neck to pull him into a searing kiss. She only lasted a second before her sharp fangs began protruding, her gums aching, eager for the soothing bite of human flesh. Caleb returned the kiss with fervor, so Geneva used her grip on him to shift his mouth down to her neck.

They stood in his massive, immaculate kitchen, Geneva's back pressed against the marble kitchen island in the center of the room. Caleb reached down to grab her thighs and lift her up so that she was sitting on the counter.

"I *do* want your body," she purred. "Badly."

Her eyes scanned his kitchen, looking for security cameras or anything that might get her caught later.

It may have been paranoia, but she couldn't take any chances. When she found nothing unusual, she pressed hers lips to Caleb's skin at the juncture of his neck and shoulder. She could feel the warmth of his blood pumping and let out a satisfied sigh as she moved her lips closer to his jugular.

His hands were all over her body, wandering at his leisure. She allowed it for a moment, enjoying his reverent touches.

Then she bared her fangs and sank them into the flesh of his neck. Caleb let out a weak whimper. Another sound exited his mouth, like he was trying to scream but didn't have the energy. His hands went slack and fell to his sides while Geneva sucked the sweet, hot liquid out of his veins.

Power coursed through her, her hunger ebbing with each drop of human blood in her system. The taste of him was so decadent and rich that she wanted to drain him entirely, and not let a single drop of him go to waste.

He gained momentary use of his hands again and tried in desperation to push himself away. Her teeth were still lodged in his neck, and she didn't want to pull away even for a second to see the look of horror on his face.

His body released further, and then he slumped to the tile floor beneath them. The twin bite marks on his neck glistened with fresh, bright red blood. The sight was so appetizing that Geneva stooped to her knees to drain that last bit of blood still coursing pitifully through his veins.

With her stomach gorged, she stood and surveilled the mess that she had made. She always made a point to not get too violent with her victims so she could save herself from a messy clean up later. Now, she had to deal with the blood on her hands and face before she could turn her attention to his body.

She washed her hands in the kitchen sink and then wiped the blood from her face and floor with a dish towel. When she was finished with the blood, she hefted Caleb's body up onto her shoulders with ease and brought him out into the spacious backyard.

Her go-to method of disposal was fire. It made the bodies harder to identify, if they could even be found after Geneva was done with them. She found a firepit on his back patio and decided it would be best to burn him in there and take the ashes with her when she was finished. So, she contorted his limp body until it fit inside the bowl-shaped pit and set it on fire.

Full and content, Geneva found a seat nearby and pulled up close to watch the flames disintegrate into the night sky. The smell of burning flesh was acrid in the air, but Caleb's house was far enough away from the others in the neighborhood that the neighbors shouldn't catch a whiff.

It took most of the evening for the body to turn to ash, and Geneva stayed perched in her lounge seat, watching him the entire time. When he had finally disappeared, and there was nothing left but a few bones and some glowing embers, Geneva scooped the hot ash into a mason jar she found in the kitchen and shoved it into her purse.

As she made her way home through the woods, she carefully sprinkled the ashes along her trail, taking zigzags and looping back around to confuse anyone who might try to track her. No one had caught her yet, or had even been suspicious of a vampire in the small town. As long as she was careful, she would be able to keep her little secret.

Once she was safely back at home, Geneva laid her head down against her pillow and closed her eyes. Vampires don't really *need* sleep, but she was tired after her big meal and wanted to take a little cat nap.

She was almost asleep when she heard the chime of her phone ringing from the depths of her purse. With a sigh, she rolled over and reached toward the floor where her purse sat and fished out her cell phone.

Luke's name flashed across the screen. She sat up and tucked her hair behind her ear. The time read five in the morning, and when she glanced out the window, she saw the sun had not yet made its morning appearance in the sky.

"Hello?" she answered, her brow furrowed in confusion.

"Good morning, Geneva," said Luke's smooth voice on the other line. "I hope I didn't wake you up."

Geneva swallowed and winced uncomfortably as she tried to sit up further on her bed. She was still wearing her black sheath dress, too exhausted to change out of it before she collapsed. Now, it felt stifling and restrictive, so she set the phone down on her bed and lifted it up over her head.

"You didn't wake me," she yelled into the receiver, tossing the dress onto the floor in the corner of the room. "I was just getting dressed, actually. What's up?"

"Well, I was about to head down to the pier to go fishing," he explained. "I thought maybe you might want to come with me."

Geneva opened her mouth to respond and found that she didn't know what to say. She had never been fishing before, nor was she interested in trying. She thought that deep down, Luke knew her aversion to such outdoor activities and was trying to test her.

"I'd love to," she replied, rising to his bait. "Let me finish getting dressed. I'll meet you at the pier in half an hour."

"I look forward to it."

Chapter Seven

Thirty minutes later, Geneva stood on the pier in the same exact spot where she had met Luke not even a month ago. The dock was silent compared to the lapping of waves on the shore. She could tell by the clean scent of the air that Luke had not arrived yet, so she sat down on the pier and hung her legs over the edge, dangling her feet above the water as she had done before.

She was wearing a simple t-shirt and skinny jeans, and her messy hair had been pulled up into a loose bun on top of her head.

By the time Luke arrived just a few minutes later, the sun was halfway up over the horizon, casting a dark orange color up into the atmosphere. Luke greeted her with a smile and extended a hand to pull her up to her feet.

"You ready?" he asked her, tugging her along toward the edge of the wharf where the boats were lined up neatly on the water.

"I've never been fishing before," she confessed.

"Yeah, I figured," Luke chuckled. "I think I can make you learn to like it, though."

Geneva gave him a sly glance. "I'm sure you can," she agreed.

When his eyes glanced back over at her, he gave her a perceptive look.

"You're an intriguing person, Geneva," he said pensively. "I'm wondering if you know what you want from me."

She blinked at him as he untied a small rowboat from the dock. His hands were sure and steady on the ropes, calloused from where he had done this so many times before. She imagined what his hands would feel like on her, and thought that maybe *that* was all that she wanted from him, at least for now.

"What makes you think I want something from you?" she asked.

He let out a snicker as he climbed into the boat

"Of course, you want something from me," he said confidently. "You want to date me? Have sex with me? Be my girlfriend?"

Geneva was startled by the questions. "We're just having fun, aren't we?" she asked.

She had been so careful not to smother him and didn't think she had given off a clingy impression. Still, Luke seemed like the type of man that women found easy to fall in love with. She wondered how many hearts he had broken over the years, and if he planned on making Geneva one of them.

"Are we?" Luke countered. "I mean, are you having fun with me?"

Geneva nodded as Luke helped her climb into the boat, and they shoved away from the shore. Luke had an oar in each hand and seemed to know exactly what to do with them to make the boat glide easily through the water.

"I'm having fun," she said. "It's just hard to figure you out. I don't know what *you* want. I just know that I like spending time with you."

Luke smiled at her with a pleasant flush on his cheeks. She wanted badly to know what he wanted from her, but she didn't think he'd be forthcoming with that information. It actually seemed like he enjoyed torturing her.

"You come off a little intense, you know," he told her. "It's like there's something really powerful behind your eyes when you look at me. I don't even know if you're doing it on purpose, but it's kind of thrilling, in a weird way."

Geneva shivered. She knew he was seeing her thirst behind her eyes, the intense hunger and craving she felt for his particularly sweet human blood. Now that she had fed recently, that intensity shouldn't be there, at least, not so obvious.

"Do you see it now?" she asked, curious.

Luke shook his head. "No, I think the idea of going fishing must have scared it out of you," he teased. "Truth be told, Geneva, I kind of like it. But I do wonder what it was that I saw. I've met a lot of people, a lot of interesting ones in my profession. None have piqued my curiosity the way you have."

Geneva hated to think that it was because of her vampirism, but she knew it had to be the truth.

"So, that's why you're interested in me," she ventured. "You're trying to figure me out."

Luke gave a nonchalant shrug.

"I'm just a regular person, Luke," she insisted. "There's nothing to figure out."

"Oh, I don't think that's true," he said. "I'm sure there's a lot more to you than you let on. For instance, your interest in me seemed to have made the prospect of fishing not so terrible. Do you really think it's worth it for a chance to hang out with me?"

Geneva gave him an insulted look.

"That's why you invited me here?" she asked accusingly. "Just to see if I would come?"

He laughed, the muscles in his broad chest flexing as he rowed them further out to sea. His dimples were showing, and the flush on his cheeks made him look happy and boyish.

"I didn't think you would," he confessed. "I was expecting you to turn me down. I guess you must really like me, huh?"

Geneva glared at him, feeling heat creep into her face.

"I'm not some kind of ditzy fool," she said. "There's nothing wrong with not liking fishing. It's not even that I don't like it!"

"Ah, you aren't ditzy," he agreed. "That much is obvious. But you *are* a bit arrogant. Do you know that? Seems like you like having men wrapped around your little finger.”

Now, it was all coming together for Geneva. She *had* been played by him. He wasn't interested in her at all. He just wanted to turn the tables on her.

“I see,” she said nonchalantly. “So, you're trying to get *me* wrapped around *your* finger, then?”

Luke laughed loudly, the sound echoing across the silent sea.

“It's not going to work,” she said to him pointedly.

“It's not going to work for you either,” he countered.

They stared at one another, the boat swaying gently beneath them. Geneva crossed her arms over her chest and let out a huff of irritation. If he was challenging her, she would gladly rise to it. She had no clue what spell she could even put on him, but she planned on unleashing everything she had.

“We'll see about that,” she said.

“I guess we will,” he replied with a smirk.

Silence settled between them. Geneva fingered at the collar of her shirt, exposing more of her skin. It was a tactic that worked well when she was just a human.

As a vampire, there was an added allure to her, the quality behind her eyes that he couldn't place. It was part of her predator biology, a certain attractive and undetectable scent that vampires released to humans.

He was still a human, a male one, however tenacious he was, so she noticed when his gaze dipped down to her newly exposed cleavage and then quickly back up to her eyes. She smirked at him and reached across the distance between them to brush his hair away from his face so she could look into his eyes. Their stormy grey color matched the murky water rocking the boat and were nearly just as beautiful.

"It'll be fun to watch you try to seduce me," he said.

"Why?" she asked coyly. "It doesn't seem like it will be that hard."

He let out a disparaging chuckle as he kept the boat moving gently through the water. When the shore had disappeared from sight, Luke fastened the oars to the boat and reached for the fishing poles he had stashed beneath their feet.

"Come here," he said, making room on his side of the boat for her to sit. "I'll show you how to hold the rod."

"I think I'm already pretty good at that," she said with a wink, but she shifted over to him nonetheless.

Beside him, she threaded her arms through his to grasp the handle of the fishing pole. His hands guided her to where they should sit, his palm warm where it rested around her. He showed her how to cast the line, and she caught on quickly. Then he showed her how to bait the worm on the hook so that it wriggled to catch the fish's attention.

"I don't know why you hate fishing so much," he said. "You don't seem grossed out by it, so what's the deal?"

Geneva wasn't grossed out by the worms or the fish, and that wasn't where her dislike of fishing stemmed from. In fact, fishing was the least gross thing she had done today. But she had always found the concept boring for the reason Luke just described. She didn't want to say that to him, though, especially since he already thought she hated all his favorite hobbies.

"You'd be really good at it. You want to know the secret to catching fish?"

Geneva nodded.

"Be quiet," he replied.

"That's it?" she asked.

"Yup," he said. "Now, we sit back and wait."

With their lines cast into the water, Luke and Geneva fell into a comfortable silence. The air was tepid around them, not too hot or too cool. As the waves swayed the boat, Geneva moved closer to Luke and rested her head against his shoulder.

She was still exhausted from her big meal with Caleb, and somewhere in the breaks of her mind, she felt a stab of guilt from it – not because she killed him, but because she hoped that Luke wouldn't find out what she had been doing earlier tonight.

He didn't seem like the jealous type, at least, not after she found out what kind of game he was trying to play with her. But she didn't want him to think of it as just a game either. She wanted him to fall in love with her. Trying to make him jealous now would only make it obvious that she was doing it for his attention.

There was another way to make Luke like her, one that was far more foolproof than jealousy. Instead of trying to play on his negative emotions, Geneva had the ability to do something even better. She could pretend to be Luke's perfect girl. He wanted a girl who loved fishing? She could be that.

After they had been sitting in silence for a few minutes, Geneva felt a tug on the line in the water.

She watched the bobber plunge beneath the surface and scramble for control of her fishing pole.

Even a shark wouldn't be strong enough to pull her into the water, but Geneva faked a struggle as she tried to reel the fish in, wavering precariously at the side of the boat until Luke came to her aid. He practically pulled her into his lap to keep her steady as his hands came to the spool over top of hers and helped her reel the fish into the boat.

A giant, flopping bass slapped onto the bottom of the rowboat. Geneva and Luke both watched it flounder for a minute before he released her in favor of removing the hook from its mouth.

"That's a big one, Geneva," he said proudly, giving her a beaming smile. "You did a great job catching your very first fish."

"Well, *you* caught it," she said, but she was still proud regardless.

He was right that it wasn't exactly unpleasant to sit out here in the calm sea and fish on an early weekend morning, away from all the bustle of life in town. Maybe Luke was onto something with his little fishing excursions.

***

Later that night, after they had each caught a few fish and released them back into the ocean, Luke walked Geneva home. The Sunday morning sun was bright in the sky now, and Geneva had never been so tired. Even though they spent little time talking in the boat and more time touching, silently enjoying each other's company, Geneva couldn't wait to get home and slide into her soft bed.

"I had a good time with you today, Geneva," Luke said as they approach her front door. "I've been in your element, and now, you've been in mine. I think we're making progress."

"You've been in my element?" she asked with a quirked brow.

"Your sister's dinner?" he ventured. "Was that not your element?"

She shook her head with a laugh. "Not at all," she replied. "Stuffy, boring dinners aren't really my scene."

Luke gave her a patronizing look. "Alright, Geneva, I'll bite," he said teasingly. "What *is* your scene?"

She shrugged nonchalantly and walked past him to unlock her front door. "I guess you'll just have to find out," she said over her shoulder.

She didn't give him a chance to respond before she pushed herself inside and slammed the door shut behind her.

Sometimes, it was better to leave him wanting more. She could feel his presence on the other side of the door, swollen with confusion. She listened intently for a moment, waiting to hear his footsteps recede from her front porch. After a few seconds, Luke walked away. Geneva sighed with relief as she made her way back into her bedroom, but she was already thinking of her next step with him.

In her bedroom, she drew the blinds and removed her clothes. As she slid into bed, she imagined Luke beside her and wondered what it would take to get him here and keep him here permanently.

Chapter Eight

A few days after her fishing adventure, Geneva stared at her blank phone screen. She had been expecting Luke to call her to see her again, but she hadn't received even a text from him since they were out on the water.

Annoyed, Geneva sat at her desk and drummed her fingers on the surface. With Luke always on her mind, it was harder for her to focus on her work. She only half-listened to what her patients had to say to her throughout the day, and by the time she was ready to leave work, she was already irritated.

She decided caffeine would pick her up at least a little bit. It helped to keep her vampiric blood circulating and curbed her cravings for blood. It even helped her skin to not be so cold to touch. As a result of all this, Meat & Greet had become one of her favorite hangout spots after work.

Her feet took her there on autopilot. She walked up to the counter at the corner to order a coffee with cream and sugar and was unsurprised to see Michael waiting there to take her order.

"Black tea?" he asked her, lifting an empty cup from the stack beside him

Geneva shook her head. "Coffee this time, please, Michael," she said. "Two sugars, one cream."

Michael gave her a skeptical look as he wrote her name and order on the cup and reached for the pot of steaming coffee sitting on the counter behind him.

"Need the extra caffeine today?" he asked with a brow raised.

Geneva nodded. "I didn't get much sleep this weekend," she confessed. "I need a little something extra to get me through this week. I'm sure I'll be back again tomorrow."

Michael lifted his gaze to make eye contact with her as he scooped a teaspoon of sugar into her cup. There was something about his gaze that Geneva found fascinating, but she had other things to focus her mind on right now.

"So, I presume things were going well with mister tall, dark, and handsome," he speculated.

Geneva let out a tiny groan of frustration.

"Not well enough," she muttered bitterly. "I think he may just be playing head games with me. It's hard to get a solid read on him, you know?"

Michael gave her a look of pity that swelled a bud of anger in her chest.

"Why put up with that?" he asked. "What's the point? Wouldn't you rather be with someone, you know, likeable?"

"He *is* likeable," Geneva insisted.

Michael handed her the cup of coffee with a sour, disbelieving look on his face.

"Is he, though? He seems like a bit of a douche."

Geneva glared at him. Feeling cocky, she snatched the cup from his hand and jutted her chin proudly into the air. She knew why he was being so petty.

"You're jealous, aren't you?" she demanded.

Michael scowled, but he couldn't hide the blush blooming on his cheeks. Even though she wasn't all that thirsty anymore, she felt her fangs prodding at her gums. It caught her off guard that Michael's blood, in that moment, was almost as appealing to her as Luke's.

"You should be happy, Geneva," he said softly. "If that guy makes you happy, then go for it. I'm not trying to stop you."

Geneva deflated, her chin drooping in defeat. He didn't rise to her bait in the same way Luke did. The difference between them was so stark, yet, they both exuded such a delightfully sweet scent. She didn't mean to hurt his feelings, but he was more sensitive than most men were. It was a weakness she could never tolerate in herself and always loathed to see in others.

Somehow, on Michael, there was something endearing about it. She felt a stab of guilt and hated the way it seemed to gnaw at her stomach, urging her to say something to rectify what she had done.

"Thank you, Michael," she said earnestly. "You're always kind to me, even when I'm a bitch."

"You're never a bitch, Geneva," he insisted.

She shrugged. "Sometimes I am."

He flashed her a smile, and she returned with a genuine grin of her own. With an abrupt but polite nod, she stepped aside to let the people lining up behind her to order. She found her usual seat in the corner of the restaurant and watched the passersby.

Her gaze was persistently drawn to Michael, and if it weren't for the flushing shame in her stomach, she would make him her next meal. She frowned, conflicted by her mixed emotions. It was hard for her to tell the difference between affection, lust, and thirst, and her thoughts felt like a jumbled mess inside her head.

Between Luke, Michael, and Caleb, Geneva had a lot of feelings to sort out. As a psychologist, it shouldn't be this hard. Yet, her vampire emotions were far more turbulent than the human equivalent. They were much more difficult to analyze.

She sat at the table, nursing at her coffee until the sun went down. By the time she left, despite all her hard thinking, she was no closer to figuring anything out.

***

Geneva reclined back in her office chair and propped her feet up onto her desk. Felix was late for his appointment with her, which wasn't like him. She watched the clock tick on the wall and drummed her fingers against the desk with boredom.

When he finally strolled into her office and took his usual seat on the couch, he was wearing a smile on his face. It wasn't like him to smile, and Geneva was happy to see some progress in his emotions as she pulled out his file.

"I apologize for being late," he said sincerely. "I ran into a nice man down at the pier, and we just started talking. Next thing I knew, three hours had gone by. You know how it is. Funny enough, he's a psychologist, just like you. I considered asking him for an appointment for a second opinion, but I kept thinking about you and eventually decided against it. You've been my counselor for years, and I hope I didn't offend you by suggesting I didn't want your help."

Geneva lifted her feet from her desk and straightened her spine.

"You met a guy at the pier?" she asked, ignoring the second half of his speech.

Felix nodded. "Pleasant fellow," he said. "Really knows his stuff when it comes to fishing. He gave me some pretty nice pointers and even offered to take me out on his boat."

"Was his name Luke by any chance?" she asked.

Felix cocked his head at her. "Yeah, you know him?" he asked. "Oh, of course, you do. He's a psychologist. Have you worked with him before?"

"Sort of," Geneva replied. "Let me guess, he's the reason for your good mood today?"

He laughed and rubbed at his brow. His posture was more relaxed than usual as he lied back against the couch. Geneva watched him with narrowed eyes, wondering if this was somehow another one of Luke's tricks, or if maybe she was reading a little bit too much into the situation.

"Maybe," Felix shrugged. "I was trying to take your advice, and well, fishing has been a good way to distract myself. I can spend hours out there on the water."

"Interesting," Geneva replied. "I've always found fishing rather boring. It gives the mind a lot of time to wander."

"I don't think that's the case at all," Felix countered. "A serenity comes over me when I'm out on the water. I enter a total state of Zen, like meditation, my mind completely freed."

"Is that why you like going fishing so much?" she asked.

He nodded at her, a crease beginning to form between his brows. He shifted up and leaned his elbows against his knees, his fingers clasped together in front of him.

"Yeah, I think so," he answered.

Geneva had always appreciated how agreeable Felix was about things, though she'd be the first to admit that the trait usually bothered her when it came to most humans. Whether consciously or not, they all sought her approval. They couldn't help it. Felix was just as entranced by her as anyone else, but his agreeability extended beyond her. She could tell by the way he spoke of his wife and son.

"Well, it sounds like you're doing much better, Felix," she said. "I'm proud. I can tell this was something you've put a lot of effort into since your last visit."

"I've been doing my best to take your advice," he said. "I'm just glad I ran into that Luke guy. He's been such a huge help."

"Yes, how fortunate," Geneva said, trying to hide the annoyance in her tone.

She couldn't help but feel like this was Luke trying to mess with her somehow. She couldn't be sure, since it didn't seem like he had influenced Felix against her, but she didn't think it was a coincidence that they ran into each other. Irritated, she quickly wrapped up the appointment with Felix and whipped out her laptop again to do some more digging on Luke's social media accounts.

There had to be something that she could find on him, something that would help her win back her vampiric edge. She must be doing something wrong to have Luke beating her at her own game. Her tricks had always worked on others in the past. It made no sense that Luke would be an exception.

As she scrolled through his socials, she found many innocuous things like she had before: his fourth-grade spelling bee championship and his high school career as a basketball star.

The only woman consistently mentioned in Luke's posts was his cousin, Lindsey, the championship bowler. Geneva could tell by their posts that the two of them grew up close and were good friends, even to this day. She clicked on Lindsey's profile out of curiosity and scrolled through her many bowling photos and margarita nights with her friends.

Eventually, she came across a post about a kidney transplant. In the post, Lindsey mentioned that she struggled with many health problems as a kid, and that the most supportive person in her life had been her cousin, Luke, who gave her a kidney when no one else in the family was a match.

The post was long, heartfelt, and sincere. It was clear that the two of them had an almost sibling-like relationship, and though Geneva knew it was insane, she felt a stab of jealously over how close she seemed to be to Luke.

Perhaps, if Geneva behaved more like Lindsey, Luke would finally take a real interest in her. It was too bold for her to just show up wherever Luke was again, but she couldn't just sit around and do nothing.

So, she formulated a plan. She would go to the bowling alley when Luke wasn't there, when there was no competition, just a practice where she knew only Lindsey would show up. If she befriended Lindsey, she could see what was so appealing about her and get closer to Luke at the same time. As she mused over the thought, she knew it sounded crazy. But she *was* a vampire, after all. Whatever form of insanity made her do these kinds of things was just part of her nature. She felt no inclination to fight it, despite knowing how it could push Luke further away.

If it paid off, it would absolutely be worth it all.

***

The next night after work, Geneva went back to the bowling alley. There weren't many people filling the lanes on a Tuesday night, so she was easily able to spot Lindsey in the far lane by herself, sipping on a beer.

She straightened the collar of her blouse and headed over to her, putting on her brightest, most cheerful smile.

"Hey," she said to Lindsey, who set down her beer as she approached.

"Hey," Lindsey replied with a bright smile of her own. The dimples must run in the family, and Lindsey's smile was bubbly and gentle. "Do I know you?"

"No, but I saw you here the other night," Geneva explained. "During the competition. You're really good."

"Thanks," Lindsey replied sincerely. "Are you a bowler, too?"

Geneva shook her head. "No, not really," she said. "I've never actually bowled before, now that I think of it. Do you think maybe you could give me a few pointers? I'm trying to learn so I can impress this guy I like, but I don't know where to start."

Lindsey beamed at those words. "That is *so* sweet," she said. "What a lucky guy. Of course, I'll teach you a trick or two. Although, I've got to tell you that bowling isn't exactly the best way to impress a man. I should know."

"I know," Geneva laughed. "This is a little different, though."

"I see," Lindsey said. "Well, grab a ball, and I'll show you how it's done. The first lesson is free, but next time, I'll have to charge you."

Geneva blinked at her and then grabbed a bowling ball from the rack.

"Are you really a professional bowler?" Geneva asked. "Like that's your job?"

Lindsey laughed. "Of course not," she said flippantly. "I mean, I *am* a professional bowler, but that's not my *job*. I'm a dental hygienist. Bowling is just… I don't know. The thing that takes the edge off. I've been pretty good at it since I was a kid. My cousin and I used to go bowling all the time when we were teenagers. It's just my thing, I guess."

"Your cousin?" Geneva asked, her curiosity piqued. She thought she would have to work Luke into the conversation, but Lindsey did the job for her.

Lindsey nodded. "We grew up practically siblings," she said. "My mom was always busy with her career, and my dad went MIA for most of my childhood. I spent a lot of time over at his house with my aunt and uncle. They always used to give us money to go to the bowling alley and get pizza on the weekends. Those are some of my fondest memories."

"How nice," Geneva said. Getting information from Lindsey would be even easier than she had originally thought. With a few more beers in her, she would tell Geneva everything she wanted to know.

"Okay, so here's how you hold the ball," Lindsey said, lifting her bright pink bowling ball so that Geneva could see how her fingers sat inside, twisted around the grips. "You need to hold it in your palm like this. Make sure the one you grabbed isn't too heavy for you."

Geneva gave her a devious look. "I think I can handle it. I *do* work out."

"Alright, alright," Lindsey laughed. "Just make sure you can swing it easily enough when you pull back. If it's too heavy, you could fall over."

"Got it," Geneva replied. "Tell me more about your cousin. You said you guys grew up close?"

"Oh, yeah. He's my best friend."

"What's he like?" Geneva pressed.

Lindsey let a nostalgic look pass over her face. Geneva watched her step up to the lane and toss the ball directly down the center. She hit a strike and smugly turned to give Geneva a proud smile.

"He's a sweet guy," she said. "Very charming and caring." She then turned her gaze to Geneva and narrowed her eyes. "Why are you so interested in him?"

"Not him," Geneva laughed. "You. You're an interesting person, Lindsey. Professional bowler *and* dental hygienist."

Lindsey blinked. "How did you know my name?"

Geneva raised a brow at her. "I remembered it from the competition," she replied. "I also noticed it monogrammed on your purse," she said, gesturing to the quilted bag sitting on the table that said *Lindsey* in bright pink thread. "I also assume that pink is your favorite color?"

An uncomfortable silence stretched between them. Geneva stared at her, waiting for her to fight or flee. Lindsey looked tense, but she relaxed as Geneva walked up to the lane and launched her bowling ball, mimicking what she had seen Lindsey do.

With her deadly aim, Geneva hit a perfect strike as well. She looked back at Lindsey to find her in shock.

"Doesn't seem like this is your first time," she accused.

"Beginner's luck," Geneva explained. "I have pretty good hand-eye coordination."

"I see," Lindsey said suspiciously. "So, what's your story? Who's this guy you're trying to impress?"

Geneva reached for another ball from the rack and gestured toward the lane for Lindsey's turn. Obediently, Lindsey trotted up to the rack to grab her ball.

"Just some guy," Geneva said vaguely. "Attractive, likes bowling. You know how it is."

Lindsey bowled another strike and then tossed a friendly glare over her shoulder. "Come on, you can be more specific than that. At least tell me your name."

"Veronica," she lied.

Lindsey laughed. "You *look* like a Veronica," she said.

"Do I look like I can be a professional bowler?" Geneva deflected, though she was amused.

Lindsey peered at her and then broke into a grin. "I get it," she said. "You must have lied to some guy and told him you were a professional bowler. Now, he wants to take you bowling, and you've got to fake the skills."

"Something like that," Geneva said as the pins were reset by the rack above the lane.

She took her place at the center, and this time, she purposefully bowled a gutter ball. Lindsey tutted in arrogant disapproval and walked up to the lane after her.

"Well, Veronica, you're kind of a knockout," she said. "I have a hard time believing *you'd* have to lie to get a man's attention. Especially about bowling."

Geneva shrugged. "Sometimes, that makes it more fun," she explained. "Like the thrill of a chase, you know what I mean?"

Lindsey shook her head. "No, I don't," she said. "That makes men sound like our prey."

"They are."

Lindsey looked at her. They held eye contact for a moment before she burst into a round of giggles. Her laugh was high-pitched and infectious, and Geneva couldn't help but smile.

"No offense, but I'd hate to be on the receiving end of your charm," Lindsey said. "You seem like a bit of a handful."

"Funny," Geneva said snidely. "I was going to say the same thing about you."

Lindsey laughed again, seemingly composed by Geneva's snarky remarks. Geneva was grateful for that because Lindsey's bubbly attitude was starting to exhaust her. The two of them continued to take turns bowling for a while with Geneva asking more questions at random, trying to not seem suspicious while she gathered information on Luke.

It wasn't until Luke walked into the bowling alley that Geneva felt the sudden need to bolt. She sensed the scent of his blood in the air immediately, before he even walked through the doors. Panic surged up in her throat. She knew he was on a date tonight with another woman, and she didn't want him to catch her with his cousin.

"Oh, look, speak of the devil," Lindsey said, pointing to the door where Luke was entering the building.

Geneva reached for her purse and slung it over her shoulder.

"I really have to get going," she said to Lindsey. "Thanks for your help today. I appreciate it. More than you know."

"Stay," Lindsey insisted. "Come meet my cousin. He's pretty decent at bowling, too. Maybe he can give you some pointers, and you can tell him why you're so fascinated with him."

Geneva shook her head vigorously.

"I've had enough for tonight, but thanks for the offer."

Before Lindsey had a chance to protest, Geneva was already gone, stolen out into the night. Stealthily, she slipped past the crowd of people and disappeared through the door.

Chapter Nine

Knowing that Luke wasn't home, Geneva decided to sneak into his house. Things were starting to take too long with him, and she needed to satisfy her cravings soon.

It wasn't hard to find his neighborhood. She could tell by his pictures on social media which part of the small town he lived in. Once she was there, it was easy to sniff out his scent. The entire street reeked of his sweet smell as she casually ambled down the road.

She came to a house on the end of the row, one meticulously well-kept with a manicured lawn and a faint fishy smell beneath the sweet, coppery tang of blood. She knew immediately that it was Luke's house. There was something about the look of it, so charming and simple.

The lock was no match for her strength, but Geneva didn't want to leave signs of breaking and entering. Instead, she climbed the gutter swiftly and silently, and crept along the roof until she came to a window.

Luke had foolishly left his window unlocked, which Geneva planned to use entirely to her advantage, but she had to make sure it was locked before she left. She didn't want anyone else breaking into his house.

The upstairs window emptied her out into a short hallway with three doors. Curious, Geneva waited a moment to listen for any signs that something alive was in the house. She didn't want to have to deal with a spirited dog or a cranky cat. But she heard nothing, so she was a little more relaxed as she headed for the first door.

She turned the handle of the knob, wincing as it rattled loudly in its old joint in the heavy brass hinges. Slowly, she eased herself inside the room and flicked the light switch on the wall. It was Luke's office, a dark, cluttered room, though it was meticulously free of dust. There were stacks of papers on the heavy oak desk in the center of the room, various psychology journals pulled from their place on the bookshelf against the wall.

Curious, Geneva perused the shelf. She found more medical journals, some self-help books, and a handful of classic fiction. Curious, she picked up a copy of Dracula and flipped through the well-worn pages. It was obviously a book he had read many times before, at least, compared to the other books on the shelf, though there was also a very loved, older edition of George Orwell's 1984.

On the desk, she found his computer, the monitor littered with symmetrically placed sticky notes. She jiggled the mouse to turn it on, but it was password protected. She could worry about getting into his computer later, but for now, she had a whole house to explore. There wasn't much else other than what she'd seen in his office, though Geneva did pause to go through the stack of patient files on his desk, looking to see if there was anything about Felix that might explain their chance meeting. Nothing.

When she finished, she slipped back out into the hall and opened the next door. This one was the bathroom, a stark and clinically white room with harsh fluorescent bulbs that made Geneva's skin tingle. As her eyes adjusted to the light, she found his medicine cabinet and searched through his various tonics and lotions.

He had a bottle of sweet-smelling aftershave, which Geneva slipped into her purse to savor later. There was also a tube of toothpaste on the counter, and Geneva was pleased to find only one toothbrush in the cup by the sink. She couldn't help but notice, however, the long blonde hair tangled in the bristles of the brush beside the toothpaste.

A little irritated, she opened all the cabinets and searched for any other signs of a woman. The only telling detail other than the long blonde hair was a pink razor she found in the shower. It could have been innocent enough, just a mix up in the pack of razors Luke bought, but something told Geneva to raise her suspicions.

She shut off the light in the bathroom and crept back out into the hall. There was only one room left upstairs. It had to be the bedroom. Geneva felt a shiver roll down her spine as she cracked the door open and peered inside.

Luke's bed was smaller than she expected, a full-size mattress on a wrought iron frame, squared in the center of the room beneath an arched window. Though it was a small room, it was beautifully decorated in dark leathers and potted plants. It smelled like cedar and Luke's sweet aftershave. Nothing about the room was feminine, much to Geneva's relief.

In fact, it seemed particularly evident that this was a *man's* bedroom. There was a vintage acoustic guitar hanging on one wall and a large television on another. The walls were painted a dark brown color, offset by the overwhelmingly green view of his backyard through the massive window.

Intrigued, Geneva peered through the window into the sprawling backyard. Luke was obviously an outdoorsy person. There was an iron firepit like Caleb's in the backyard, surrounded by low cushions and more potted plants. He also seemed to like leafy ferns and the angular lines of snake plants and cacti. It gave the place a jungle forest feel, an overgrown and wild energy.

She returned her attention to the bedroom, admiring the dark silk sheets, the pristine way they were folded around the mattress. He put an obvious effort into keeping his home tidy, which turned Geneva on even more. She was used to thinking of men as grown children in need of coddling and pampering. If Eugenia's husband, Parker, was any indication, the lot of them were lazy slobs, regardless of how prestigious they were in their careers.

Luke was different, though. He was a man who had every aspect of his life together. He was smart, capable, charming, clean, well-spoken, an endless list of qualities that made him the perfect match for Geneva. The findings in his house only solidified that so far, though she still couldn't get that blonde hair out of her mind.

Again, she slipped silently out into the hall, making sure to shut off the lights and close the door exactly the way she had found it. The stairs were a rickety, uncarpeted wood that creaked even under Geneva's supernaturally light footsteps. When she got to the bottom, she was facing the front door, with the dining room on her left and the kitchen on her right. Past the stairs behind her was a walkway into the living room. Geneva made her way there first, curious about his living habits.

There was no television in the room, much to her surprise. Instead, there was a large, illuminated fish tank that took up nearly half the wall. Curious, Geneva moved closer to inspect it, weaving her way through the mismatched chairs and chesterfield sofa.

The tank was filled with colorful tropical fish, yellows and blues and pinks, glimmering in the eerie green light that dappled by the water. The house was silent compared to the drone of the water tank and the chime of the filter of bubbles coming through a tube at the top. Geneva smiled, wondering how Luke had chosen these specific fish for his tank.

It seemed that his hobby wasn't merely fishing, but actually fish themselves. Beside the fish tank, she found a stack of books about aquarium fish and a few bottles of fish feed. Though she couldn't say that she was fond of either fish or fishing, Geneva liked that Luke had such interesting hobbies that he was truly passionate about.

An aquarium was a date she didn't necessarily mind going on. She wouldn't have to get her hands dirty for that, and she might even enjoy it. She would be out of the sun, and there would be lots of opportunities for her to get physically closer to Luke.

Tucking that tidbit of information away for later, Geneva glanced around the rest of the living room. There was an unfinished Rubik's cube on the coffee table and a pair of nail trimmers sitting on the edge of the couch. Otherwise, the room was immaculate, not a speck of dust or an unfluffed pillow in sight.

Geneva then moved into the kitchen, a charming farmhouse-style kitchenette with battered pots and pans hanging from the ceiling. This room, too, was taken over by potted plants, aloe on the counter, basil and mint growing on the windowsill, and a large philodendron climbing down the side of the stainless-steel refrigerator.

She pulled the refrigerator door open and peered at its contents. There wasn't much food, but there were cases of beer and jars of pickles. He could try to hide it, but he was still a man, through and through. If she were his girlfriend, the first thing she would do is take him to the grocery store and stock his kitchen with some healthy food.

Just to be sure there weren't anything suspicious, she went through his cabinets and pantry, unimpressed with his cheap China and sugary breakfast cereals. She even peeked into the trash to find empty beer bottles and fish bones, presumably from meals he had caught himself. At least, he was self-sufficient.

The dining room was unremarkable, largely because it appeared to be unused. There was the thinnest layer of dust coating the antique table, and the closed drapes looked as though they'd never been opened.

Having explored the entire house, Geneva still wasn't quite ready to leave. There was something comforting about being in his home, though she wished that he would've invited her instead of her having to sneak in. It was a silly myth that vampires could not enter a home without being invited, but the fact that she still had to fish for an invitation seemed oddly poetic.

She climbed the stairs again and went back into his bedroom. It already smelled the most like him in here, but she reached into her purse anyway to grab his bottle of aftershave. She dabbed a little of it on her wrist and climbed into his bed, beneath the thick wine-colored duvet. Content, she heaved a deep sigh and settled against his pillows.

One day, she would be here with Luke beside her. She would have liked for that to be sooner rather than later, but she just couldn't understand why he wasn't obsessed with her like most men were.

Unlike most men, Geneva actually wanted to be close to Luke. She wanted him to like her because *she* liked *him*. Despite what her sister thought, it wasn't normal for her to get these kinds of feelings for a person. The need to be close to Luke was always on her mind, no matter what was going on.

She thought of him still at the bowling alley with his cousin and wondered if Lindsey had mentioned her to him. Hopefully, the fake name she had given her would be enough to keep Lindsey from spilling the truth. She was worried that Lindsey was too suspicious of her already, and if Geneva wanted to be with him long-term, then she'd have to get along with Lindsey.

She also worried that Luke would find out about the covert snooping she had done, but somehow, she was thrilled by the idea of getting caught in his bed. Would he be angry? Would he like it? Would it be a funny story to the start of their future together?

The scent of him was powerful in the air, so strong she almost believed that he was here. She sighed as she settled deeper into the sheets, relishing the idea that she might one day curl up beside him here.

Suddenly, she heard the sound of the garage door roaring open. Instantly alert, she sat up and sloppily made the bed. She could hear thudding footsteps in the kitchen as she slipped back out into the hallway and headed toward the window. It was still open, though not wide enough for her to fit through. Carefully, so as to not make a sound, Geneva pushed it up just far enough to squeeze her body through so that she was back on the roof.

Below her in the driveway, Geneva spotted a suspicious head of blonde hair getting out of a black corvette. She knew that was not Luke's usual sedan, which was parked in the garage now. She could barely see the tail end of it from her perch on the roof.

As silently as she could, Geneva slid the window down and made sure the latch hook would lock as it fell shut. Then she carefully crept into the shadows on the roof, staying just far enough out of sight that she could still see the woman below.

She was dressed in a tight pink dress and matching heels, the antithesis of Geneva's entire aesthetic. Everything about her was bubbly and pink, and it reminded her of Lindsey in a way that disgusted her. Of course, Luke had a type, even if he didn't know what it was.

Geneva wondered if Luke ever saw anything in her at all, or if it was just her vampirism that endeared her to him. She was nothing like the women he seemed to date, and he had all but admitted that he found something about her mysteriously intriguing.

She watched the woman walk into the garage and overheard the beginnings of a steamy conversation between her and Luke. Unsettled and irritated, Geneva leapt down from the roof and onto the grass lawn beside the house.

Now that she knew for certain there was at least one other woman in the picture, Geneva needed to figure out a way to get rid of her. Once she was sure the woman and Luke had both gone inside the house, Geneva found herself standing at the driver side of the black corvette.

The poor fool had left her car unlocked, so Geneva climbed into the driver's seat and began rifling through the woman's possessions. There was a high-end lip gloss in the cupholder and a pair of trendy sunglasses tucked into the sun visor. Otherwise, the car was empty and relatively clean other than a bit of grass on the mats.

Geneva opened the glovebox and looked through the woman's insurance information for her name. Holly Puckett. She sounded like she would make an excellent snack later. Geneva wasn't keen on drinking female blood, but she could make an exception this one time. She placed everything back as she had found it in the car and shut the door as quietly as she could before slipping back out into the dark night.

She went straight home, her blood pulsing through her veins. Jealousy made the natural aggression in her surface, tugging her fangs down out of her gums. She shook her head, trying to clear her mind and suppress the violent urges in her head. They weren't usually so hard to control, but when she thought of Holly sleeping in Luke's bed, using his brush, kissing him… it fueled the burgeoning bloodlust brewing in her gut.

Too cunning to blindly attack, Geneva conceived a plan once she was back in her own bedroom and had changed into a more comfortable sweatshirt and shorts to wear. She couldn't let Luke get distracted by little Lindsey clones who were only going to hurt him in the end. As a psychologist himself, he should have been able to see the deep cycle he was in.

Luke was a man who liked to take care of others, and Lindsey had been under his care since they were kids. It was only natural that he would be drawn to others he could take care of, moronic blondes included.

Geneva wouldn't have to play the ditzy damsel in distress to get Luke's attention. She had another tool at her disposal: their common career goals. It gave her the perfect excuse to need Luke's help and still maintain her dignity.

But she needed to get Holly out of the way first, so as she slid into bed, Geneva opened her laptop and did a little digging on Holly Puckett. Just a simple search of her name brought up a plethora of social media pages, each one filled with picture after picture of her long-legged bikini shots and heavily edited selfies.

Annoyed that Luke could find someone like this appealing, Geneva scrolled through until she found Holly's basic information page. She was nearly a decade younger than Geneva and Luke, and she worked as a waitress at the drive-in diner where the servers all wore roller skates and old-fashioned poodle skirts. Her dreams were to become a famous singer and actress, though Geneva thought that unlikely in this small hick town.

However, upon further scrolling, Geneva found that Holly would be performing in a Shakespeare on the Square play next weekend. That meant that her disappearance would be noticed.

Just because Geneva was careful about her kills didn't mean she could kill without consequences. Eventually, the bodies would start to pile up. People would catch on to the fact that people were missing or dead. If Holly's death was going to get noticed, Geneva would have to find a way to make sure that no one would care. If she made it look like Holly ran away, no one would even go looking for her.

She had to drive Holly away from the play, make her quit her role or get fired from it. By then, Geneva would have terrorized her enough that her blood would be ripe and sour, a potent and delicious kind of zing she didn't usually get to taste from the brave and aroused men she often fed from. It wasn't her favorite flavor, by any means, but it would be a satisfying meal nonetheless.

Feeling a little bit better, Geneva shut her laptop and pulled the covers up to her chin. There was no reason to panic just because Luke got distracted. She still had a chance to set things right again. She just needed to take care of Holly first.

Chapter Ten

Geneva was a bitter mess in the days following the discovery of Holly. She didn't want to think her hold on Luke was weak, but she was at a loss for how to strengthen it. She wracked her brain for an appropriate work problem to ask him. He specialized in phobias if she remembered correctly. She thought, perhaps, she could take to him a problem of a made-up patient with a major phobia of commitment. It perfectly meshed her specialty with his, but it was a little too direct for Geneva to feel comfortable with.

She also felt it was probably a good idea to give him a little more space. While she knew that Luke was clearly not thinking about her, she also knew that absence made the heart grow fonder. Time apart might give them a chance to miss each other.

So, she laid low for a few weeks. She went to work and handled her patients, went to see a movie with her sister, and spent some time at Meat & Greet, researching more about Luke on her laptop.

The night before the first Shakespeare on the Square play was scheduled, Geneva decided to pay Holly Puckett a visit. Using her pictures on social media, it wasn't hard to figure out that Holly spent most of her time at the mall and the diner where she worked.

Geneva made her way to the mall, hoping she would be able to spot Holly there. That would be the perfect place to break her self-esteem and send her running for the hills. By the time Geneva was finished with her, she wouldn't want to go anywhere near a stage or camera.

She found the blonde woman in the company of a few friends, walking through the food court, each with an iced coffee in hand. Geneva listened to their shallow chatter as she sneakily followed them through the mall.

Holly and her friends all seemed to have bubbly, infectious laughter and beaming personalities. It annoyed her trying to keep up with them as they wandered through the mall. She wondered how people had the energy to be around her. Holly talked a mile and minute, and Geneva had long given up on eavesdropping on the conversation.

Eventually, the three of them walked into a boutique where the walls were lined with flared skirts and puff-sleeved dresses, as racks of homemade leatherwear filled the air with the warm, earthy smell of polished leather.

One of the girls reached for a leather cowboy hat and perched it atop her dainty head. The girls busted into a round of giggles as it slipped down to cover her eyes.

"Oh, look at this dress," Holly said, reaching for a sky-blue dress hanging on the wall.

She pulled it down from the rack and held it up to her body for her friends' approval. It was a hideous floral prairie dress in a pastel robin's egg color that made Geneva want to vomit. The girls cooed and awed over it while Geneva busied herself with absently flipping through the hangers on a nearby rack.

"I think I should get this for my date with Luke next week," she continued, posing with the dress draped against her in the mirror. "Blue's his favorite color."

Geneva scowled with irritation. She wasn't sure she believed that blue was Luke's color. It was far more likely for it to be red, like Geneva's. Men loved the color red, and Geneva was, well, suited for the color.

But she had to admit that the pretty blue color of the dress *did* match Holly's eyes perfectly and seemed to suit her skin tone well. She would look pretty in the dress, but fortunately for Geneva, Luke would never see her in it.

She followed Holly and her friends around the mall until they parted ways in the food court. When she was alone, Holly wandered into a department store, her arms laden with shopping bags. She almost made too easy a target.

Geneva approached her as she was eyeing sheath dresses on the rack. She ran her fingers over a green suede one and let out a wistful sigh.

"That color would never suit you," Geneva said, reaching out to touch the fabric beside the place where Holly was holding it. "The style isn't right for you either," she continued, basking in the look of mortification on Holly's face.

"You're right," Holly said with terse politeness. "It doesn't go with my coloring very well."

Geneva nodded. "Glad we agree," she said, "but not just the coloring. I'm amazed that you'd even have the confidence to wear what you've got on, you know, with those wide hips. At least, they're balanced out by your broad shoulders."

Holly gaped at her, redness swallowing her cheeks. She let out an indignant scoff and turned her shoulder sharply, jostling the collection of shopping bags attached to her arm.

"I didn't mean to offend you," Geneva said. "I just wanted to say that I admire your confidence. You have a lot of bravery to put yourself out there like that."

"Like what exactly?" Holly asked, tossing a glare at Geneva over her shoulder.

Geneva swallowed. She didn't need Holly to be angry. She needed her to be self-conscious. In her plans, Geneva hadn't accounted for the girl's healthy self-esteem.

"It's nothing," Geneva assured her. "I'm sorry. I didn't mean anything by it. You're perfectly fine."

That seemed to do the trick. Holly's brow creased. She shifted her shopping bags in her arms and gave a longing glance at the olive-green sheath dress again. Then she turned her gaze back to Geneva, her cheeks burning and eyes narrowed to slits.

"You should really work on your manners," she said primly, squaring her shoulders at Geneva with false bravado if the scent of her blood had anything to say about it.

There was a sweet but tangy quality to the scent that let Geneva know she had successfully gotten under Holly's skin.

"Yeah, I've heard that before," Geneva drawled.

There was one last piece to the plan, and Geneva would be in the clear to kill her. She watched the poor girl scurry away, clutching her shopping bags to her chest. Since Holly wasn't particularly aware of her surroundings or protective of her belongings, it had been easy for Geneva to sneak her hand into the woman's purse and snatch her planner.

When Holly was out of sight, Geneva flipped through her schedule and looked for the next fitting date for her costume. There was one final fitting tomorrow, two days before the first show. It seemed she had the role of Miranda in Shakespeare's *The Tempest*. Her dress had to be Geneva's next target.

She wasn't a particularly skilled seamstress, but Geneva knew how to take in a dress. All she had to do was sneak into the tailor's shop and make a quick alteration. When her dress turns out to be too small, Holly would feel far too self-conscious to go on stage.

Holly had marked the tailor's address in her planner, so Geneva headed straight there. She didn't have a lot of time left to alter the dress, and she wanted to make sure it would fit a little too snug. She had a pretty accurate idea of Holly's size, so all she had to do was tighten the dress up just a little.

When she walked into the tailor's shop just a few blocks down from the mall, there was an old woman behind the counter. She was stationed in front of a cluttered mess of fabric, thread, and beads, her head buried in the busy work. She barely glanced up as the bell above the door chimed to announce Geneva's arrival.

"I'll be with you in just a moment," the woman said, adjusting her bifocals on the bridge of her nose.

"Take your time," Geneva replied, wandering through the messy shopfront. The garments weren't on display so much as they were haphazardly strewn through the tiny square footage of the room, half-finished and hanging limply from mannequins or draped across console tables.

Geneva found a corner of the room that appeared to be designated for costumes. There were all kinds of colorful fairy dresses and a delightfully small Peter Pan outfit. Amongst the outlandish pieces, Geneva spotted a dark blue renaissance dress with gilded trim. She glanced back at the old woman to make sure she wasn't looking before she lifted the hem of the dress and found the customer tag.

Holly's name was scrawled in untidy loops of penmanship on the tag. Stealthily, Geneva lifted the dress and rolled it around her hand to make it small enough to fit into her purse. She shoved it inside, cramming the extra fabric down so it wouldn't get caught in the zipper.

"You're obviously busy," Geneva called out as she quickly made her way to the door. "I'll come back another time."

She didn't give the old woman a chance to respond before she was out the door with the dress. It made her feel giddy to have it packed into her purse. Though it was nothing that she couldn't have done without her vampiric skills, there was something as equally thrilling about the small crime as there was about biting into human flesh.

Geneva made her way home swiftly and pulled out her sewing kit from the back of her closet. It had been a while since she touched needle and thread, but it came flooding back to her as she removed the seams on the back of the dress and folded the fabric in to make it tighter. It was just a couple of simple stitches up the back on either side of the zipper to put it all together.

It did, however, take her longer than she had expected. The shop was closed by the time she finished, and the sky had grown dark.

As she was getting ready to go to bed, she heard her phone begin to ring. Thinking it might be Luke, she rushed to grab it from where it sat on the kitchen counter. Instead, it was Eugenia's name that flashed across the screen, so Geneva dropped her phone back on the marble counter with a groan of irritation.

She wasn't in the mood to deal with Eugenia's do-gooder attitude. She didn't want her sister to know what she had done to Holly, but she didn't think she would be able to keep her mind off the ordeal either.

Ignoring Eugenia's call, Geneva went to bed, feeling a strange mixture of guilt and glee.

***

The next day, Geneva replaced the dress. It was much easier than she'd thought to walk right into the shop with the dress stuffed into her purse and walk right out empty-handed. It was a shame that she wouldn't be able to see the look on Holly's face when she tried on the dress and found the fabric too tight for her to squeeze into.

As she walked down the street, delighted by her success, she felt a sudden and strong notion that she missed Luke. It had been too long since she'd seen him, and she wanted to feel close to him again.

He was probably at work, where she should have been. She had to move several of her appointments around to deal with the Holly situation, and they could wait a little longer. She needed a Luke fix, and she knew exactly how to get one.

Luke's computer was bound to have his schedule on it. From there, she could see his emails and maybe even hack into his phone. Then she could know where he was at all times and get a better understanding of her prey.

She went back to Luke's house, wearing her jogging shorts and a sports bra. If anyone found her in the neighborhood, she could pass off as a lost cardio bunny. It was easy to retrace her steps back to his house, and when she came to his front door, this time, she had no problem twisting the knob until it broke, and the door swung open easily on its hinges.

The window upstairs was likely still locked, and if she fixed the doorknob just right, she could make it seem like Luke broke it when he tried to turn it.

She headed straight for his office and jiggled the mouse on his computer. The screen lit up with Luke's name and a little picture of a bucket hat with a fishing hook threaded through the brim. Beneath it, the cursor for the password blinked at her.

There were a few fishing- and bowling-related passwords that she tried before she gave up, afraid that she would lock herself out for good. Instead, she started pilfering through his desk, looking for a sticky note or something that he might have written his password down on. Luckily, she came across a notepad in the second drawer of the desk with a series of usernames and passwords written down.

That's stupid of him, Geneva thought, but she appreciated that he made it so easy for her. To her dismay, the first password on the list, Lindseybear2, was the one that unlocked his computer for her. Geneva scoffed with disgust before she opened up his files.

There were mostly work-related things on his computer, patient files and tax records. There were no video games or secret pornography stashes that Geneva could find. She opened up the calendar app and glanced at his upcoming schedule. She was annoyed to find that he planned to attend Holly's play this weekend.

Another date was planned with her the weekend after that, a fact that stung Geneva's skin and made her feel flushed. He seemed to want to spend a lot of time with this Holly chick, and not enough time with Geneva.

She synched her phone to his calendar so that she would be able to see what he was up to at all times. Then she did another cursory sweep of his computer, just to make sure she didn't miss anything important or suspicious.

When she was finished, she made sure to adjust the doorknob just right so that it wouldn't appear broken until he grabbed it. Then she headed downtown to get some food before she went into work for the day.

Michael wasn't behind the coffee counter when she walked into Meat & Greet, which for some reason, disappointed her. She ordered a small coffee and a burger combo from the pimply teenager behind the counter and then made her way to the office.

To her surprise, when she got to the office, the receptionist told her she had a missed call from

Luke. There was a voicemail on her answering machine, the red light blinking at her as she sat down at her desk and picked up the receiver.

"Hey, Geneva, it's Luke," he said in the voicemail, his tone clinical and professional. "I have a patient I want to refer to you. He has a fear of intimacy, and that's getting in the way of his relationship with his wife. I was wondering if that was something you'd be interested in handling for me. Give me a call back when you get a chance."

Geneva pursed her lips as she hung up the receiver. She couldn't help but smile at the way he had added the *for him* part in there, like he was asking her for a favor rather than giving her work to do. She wasn't all that interested in taking on his patient, but for all she knew, this was Luke's way of getting closer to her. After all, she *had* thought the same thing already.

So, on her cell, she called Luke back.

"Hello?"

"Good morning, Luke," she said, her voice as bright and cheery as she could make it.

"It's the afternoon, I think," he said good-naturedly. "Busy day?"

"Something like that," Geneva replied. "My receptionist told me I missed your call. What can I help you with?"

Geneva heard a feminine giggle in the background on the other line, and her stomach twinged with dread. According to his schedule, he was still at the office, but that didn't mean he couldn't invite Holly over for an illicit visit.

"My patient, Baxter Chase," Luke said, ignoring the giggle. "He's terrified of intimacy, and part of overcoming that fear for him is trusting his partner, which I don't think he does. That's really more your area of expertise than mine, so I was wondering if you could help."

"Of course," Geneva replied, swallowing the dryness in her throat. "Tell him to give me a call. I'll see if I can help."

"Good," Luke whispered, sounding relieved. "Listen, I'd love to stay and chat, but I've got to get going. Lots of patients to see today."

"Sure," Geneva replied. "I understand."

"Goodbye, Geneva."

"Goodbye, Luke."

The line went silent. Geneva stared at her phone, unsure of whether or not that was a ruse. He seemed too genuine on the phone. He hadn't flirted with or teased her, and it sounded like he was sending an actual patient her way. Maybe he had been serious.

Geneva was irritated for the remainder of the work day, snapping at patients or cutting her appointments short to sulk bitterly in the solitude of her office. When she left for the day, she went back to Meat & Greet, hoping to run into Michael.

He was one of the few people who didn't seem aggressively judgmental of her, and even though he might not support her decisions, he never made her feel bad because of them. She was dying to talk about Luke and Holly, and Michael was the only person she could think of to talk about things like that with.

Sometimes, it bothered her that she didn't have many friends, certainly not as many as Eugenia had. Geneva had always been a loner, even before she was turned into a vampire. She was introverted, though she was also confident in herself. She didn't think there was anything wrong with her, but sometimes, she found it hard to stave off the loneliness.

Michael was standing by the coffee corner when she arrived, much to her relief. The afternoon crowd was sparse, which meant she would actually have a chance to have a conversation with him.

She waited in the short line, and when she got to the counter, Michael already had a tea with cream and sugar brewed for her. He handed it to her with a smile.

"I wondered when I'd see you again," he said.

"And here I am," she replied, reaching for her wallet to pay for the tea.

"I'm about to take my break," he told her as he swiped her credit card. "Would you mind some company?"

"Not at all," Geneva said with relief. "I'd love some, actually."

"Rough time in the romance department?" he asked.

The two of them made their way back to the corner table as Michael pulled his apron over his head. He pulled out her chair for her, and Geneva obligingly sat down.

"Sort of," she explained. "I think Luke is seeing another woman."

"Oh," Michael said lamely, inspecting his fingernails. "So, does that mean you're ready to give up and move on?"

Geneva vehemently shook her head. "Never," she said. "Luke is *mine*. You'll see. I just need to figure out a way to draw him back in."

"What if he's happier with this other woman, though?" Michael asked. "Why would you want to take that away from him?"

Geneva scoffed at him with disdain. She often told her patients to prioritize their spouse's happiness, but never over their own. Geneva would be much happier with Luke, and Luke just didn't understand how happy he could be with her yet.

"Luke isn't happy with that blonde bimbo," Geneva snapped.

Michael was slightly taken aback. "Have you met this woman?" he asked her suspiciously. "Why so judgmental?"

Geneva fought against the urge to roll her eyes.

"I *have* met her, actually," Geneva replied. "She's tacky, and a bit of a brat."

Michael scoffed.

"It's true," she said defensively, crossing her arms over her chest.

"I'm sure that's not true," Michael insisted. "You're just being jealous. Can you step back for a moment to think clearly? Come on, Geneva, you're a psychologist."

Geneva blinked indignantly at him, her fangs piercing through her gums. Now Michael, too, was irritating her. Was there anywhere else to turn?

"Geneva, don't give me that look," Michael said. "Be honest with me. You're jealous, aren't you?"

"Of course, I'm jealous, Michael. What kind of dumb question is that?" she asked snidely. "Why is he interested in that moron but not me? I'm so much more interesting, smarter, and I know damn well that I'm sexy. I can't figure out why he would choose her over me."

Michael gaped at her and then let out a pleased but still incensed sneer. "I think I know why," he said. "You're kind of abrasive and arrogant."

Shocked, Geneva shut her mouth.

"You feel very deeply for Luke, and I find that admirable," Michael continued, "but you're letting your emotions cloud your judgment in a really heinous way. Seriously, Geneva, how exactly did you meet her again?"

Self-consciously, Geneva crossed her arms over her chest.

"I ran into her at the mall."

Michael eyed her with suspicion.

"I think you're lying to me," he said, "but I'm not going to press you. I wish I could just shake you and make you see how silly you're being. There are so many other guys out there who would be a much better match for you."

"Guys like *you?*" she teased.

Michael looked stung. Geneva had the decency to feel ashamed of herself. Surely, Michael didn't think he actually had a chance with her.

"If you're suggesting that *I'm* jealous, I'd think again if I were you," Michael said, his voice low and steely. "I *do* like you, Geneva, but it doesn't matter to me who you end up with. As long as you are happy. I think you should take a while to think about if Luke would actually make you happy, or if it's just the idea of him that you like so much."

Abruptly, Geneva got up to her feet.

"No, come on, Geneva, don't be mad," Michael said, reaching for her hand.

He tugged at her arm, and Geneva relented. She felt personally attacked when she had only wanted a safe place to vent her frustration. The feeling of Michael's warm hand around her wrist convinced her to stay. His pleading brown eyes didn't hurt either.

"What makes you think you're so wise, Michael?" she demanded. "Why do you think you've got it all figured out?"

Michael laughed. "I don't have it all figured out," he said. "I just prioritize what's important to me. As far as you're concerned, I want you to be happy.

Anything I say to you is in earnest pursuit of that, and I'm sorry if my bluntness offended you."

"Michael, that's naïve," she replied. "You don't want me to be happy. You want me to be happy *with you*."

To her surprise, he looked angry instead of ashamed. She expected him to blush and look away, but the glow on his face was much different.

"You won't be happy with anyone, Geneva. Not until you do some serious self-reflection."

He shoved his chair away from the table and stood up. Geneva watched him hook his apron over his neck and tie it, his motions calm despite his obvious irritation. She almost admired how in control of it he seemed. He didn't lash out at her, though his scathing words made her stomach feel nauseous.

She didn't want to leave things upended and precarious like this, so when he started to walk away, she called after him.

"Michael, wait," she said. "Maybe you're right. I'll think about it some more."

Michael gave her a skeptical look, and she didn't blame him because she didn't mean a single word she had just said. But it still unsettled her to leave with Michael angry at her.

"I've got to get back to work, Geneva."

Hurt, she dropped her hands onto her lap and sighed. It seemed that not even Michael was a safe place for her. Quickly, she finished her tea and headed back out to the street. She didn't want to linger in front of him longer than she had to. It was already humiliating enough to be chastised by him in front of an audience.

She went home, defeated, and crawled into bed. There was no reason for her to feel so badly when her plan was on track to succeed, but the loneliness of it all was upsetting. She could only hope that once things all worked out, she would have Luke by her side to stave off the loneliness.

Chapter Eleven

Geneva woke up the morning of Holly's final dress fitting with a smile on her face. Tonight, would be the night she finally gets her blood. She rushed through her appointments at work so that she could be waiting outside the tailor when Holly came out.

Holly's face was wet with tears when she left the tailors, though she had her composure. Geneva couldn't hear more than a sniffle from her as she walked across the street toward the apartment complexes and townhouses. Geneva followed her from the other side of the street, keeping to the shadows and blending into the crowd.

When they finally came to a run-down apartment toward the back of the complex, Geneva watched Holly enter and then scoped out the windows and backdoor to see her best point of entry.

All of them were locked, a fact which she admired Holly for. She was a woman, and probably more scared of intruders than Luke was. It was smart of her to lock the windows, but the locks were no match for Geneva's strength.

She popped a lock on the kitchen window with a firm tug and slid it open. She could hear Holly sobbing in the other room, her composure lost now that she was in the privacy of her own home. Geneva crept through the cluttered kitchen, disgusted by the empty salad containers and snack cake wrappers littered around. This woman was no good for Luke. She couldn't even keep her own house clean.

Holly was draped dramatically over the couch, her face buried in the cushion. It allowed Geneva to creep into the room unseen and unheard. She sat down on the armchair across from Holly and watched her for a moment, feeling slightly sorry for her. Soon, she would be put out of her misery entirely.

"You're not right for him, you know," Geneva said.

Holly screamed and reeled up into a sitting position, clutching a pillow to her chest. Her eyes fell on Geneva, wide and frightened. Then a seething anger settled onto her face.

"You," she spat. "What are you doing in my house?"

"I think you should leave this town and never come back," Geneva said.

Holly rolled her eyes and reached for her purse on the coffee table. "I'm calling the cops," she screamed, tossing a nasty glare in Geneva's direction.

Geneva snatched her purse before she could grab it and tossed it to the other side of the room. Holly fell back onto the sofa, the anger melting into fear, and Geneva stepped closer.

"You're a fat slob," Geneva accused, lowering herself to sit on the coffee table, her knee brushing against Holly's. "Don't you think Luke deserves better than a fat slob? You can primp and preen however much you want, but you're still just a pig wearing lipstick."

Tears began to stream from Holly's face. She tried to get up from the couch, but Geneva pushed her down with an unnecessarily rough shove.

"So, you're going to leave town, understood?" Geneva commanded. "You'll tell Luke you don't want to see him anymore, and you'll move to some other town where you can lose weight and learn how to clean up after yourself."

Holly whimpered as Geneva applied more pressure to her shoulder to keep her from standing up.

"Who the hell are you?" she demanded, trying to twist out of Geneva's grasp.

"Someone you want to listen to," Geneva warned. "Now, pack your things."

Holly shook her head in denial. "You can't be serious. I have to perform in a play—"

"You know damn well you won't be performing in any play," Geneva interrupted. "No one wants to see that. Start packing before I hurt you. And while you're at it, try to collect yourself. You're going to have to call Luke in a minute, and you can't be a blubbering mess on the phone."

Geneva gripped Holly's shoulder with force, tight enough to make her cry out in pain as she shoved her up to her feet toward the bedroom. Holly looked back at Geneva over her shoulder like she wanted to protest, but then she thought better of it.

She scuttled into the bedroom and began to pull hangers of clothes out of her closet. The poor fool really believed that Geneva was going to just let her go. She made a fairly valiant effort to cease her crying and get a suitcase packed while Geneva watched with narrowed eyes, savoring the scent of fear in the air around her.

Geneva pulled Holly's phone out of her purse and made her unlock it. Holly started to protest, but when Geneva bared her fangs, she slunk back against the wall, a cowering, quivering mess.

She abandoned all pretense of packing to huddle herself in the corner, her composure once again wrecked. Maybe she wouldn't be able to call Luke today. Perhaps a text would have to do.

There was a long chain of texts between Holly and Luke on the phone. It was a lot of flirting and idle chat, the kind of talk that made Geneva cringe. Surely, Luke wasn't into this bland, unappealing conversation from this silly, vapid little girl.

Yet, his heart emojis and consistent replies told another story. Hurt and annoyed, Geneva began typing, her thumbs flying furiously across the screen.

"Luke," she spoke as she wrote. "I'm moving to Nebraska. I have to spend some time working on myself. I'm sure you understand. I hope you'll meet a woman who makes you truly happy."

She pressed send and then blocked Luke's number so he couldn't reply. Then she turned her gaze to Holly, who had gained the courage to try and slip back into the living room. Just as she was creeping closer to the door, Geneva shot across the room and caught her by the arm.

"I'm sorry, Holly, but you brought this on yourself," Geneva said regretfully.

Then she twisted Holly by the arm until she had access to the junction between her neck and shoulder, and Geneva sank her fangs into the poor woman's flesh. She let out a high-pitched squeal that faltered when Geneva bit down harder.

Her blood was coppery and sour, ripe with fear, hatred, and confusion. Geneva drank greedily from her warm flesh, savoring every drop of her hot blood. Her screams fizzled into slow, pained gurgles. As Geneva drained the last bit of blood, Holly's body slumped to the ground at her feet.

The hunger thrumming in Geneva's veins faded. She wiped her mouth on the back of her hand and licked, careful not to waste any blood. It just made more of a mess for her to clean up later. And there was already a big enough mess.

Hopefully, the text message to Luke would be enough to throw the cops off Holly's disappearance. Now, she just had to find a place to stash the body. It never seemed to get any easier, no matter how many times she'd done it.

This time, instead of burning the body, she decided to throw it into the ocean. It was a much faster way of permanently disposing it than incineration, as long as she weighted it well enough so that it wouldn't float back up to the surface.

Only, it wouldn't be so easy to sneak a human body out of the apartment complex. She had walked, and didn't have her car with her, which was a nuisance most of the time. Still, she was glad it wasn't here to incriminate her.

That meant she was going to have to get creative. So, Geneva found a small but ornate cabinet with latched doors. The inside was filled with a slew of DVDs and some old college textbooks. Geneva tossed them all from the cabinet and sized it up, wondering if Holly's body would fit inside.

Despite Geneva's heckling, the woman *was* small enough to fit inside if Geneva folded her limbs just right. Though it was heavy with Holly's body, it wasn't heavy enough to hold her to the ocean floor yet.

She searched Holly's apartment, looking for things that were small and heavy. She pushed a few cast-iron pots into the cabinet alongside a small but heavy silver bowl and some cans of tomato soup. She also stuffed some blankets and sheets wherever there was space left, leaving no room for anything to get jostled around inside.

Then, the hard part. She could easily feign that the cabinet was light and empty if she lugged it across the apartment complex. It could simply pass as a woman buying a piece of furniture or moving to a new place.

But Geneva's experience told her that men would come to her aid if they saw her carrying an unwieldy piece of furniture by herself. She'd have to be quick, but not suspicious, until she made it to the woods on the other side of the mall. From there, she could break into a run and be at the pier in no time.

And so, with her plan in mind, she carried the cabinet out onto the street, holding it against her hip so people would think it was light enough for her to carry by herself. Carefully, she made her way through the pedestrian crowd, plastering a fake smile on her face.

When she finally made it to the space behind the mall, where trucks unloaded their cargo, she broke into a run. The pier wasn't too far away, but she was sweating with exhaustion, not from the heavy load, but from having to blend in and appear normal. She was sick of her life always being like this, dodging and sneaking around.

But it had to be done. She lugged the cabinet down to the pier and heaved it onto a rowboat tied up at the docks. Fishermen were often leaving things unattended in this small town, which was one reason living here worked so well to her benefit.

Remembering the way Luke had rowed the boat out to sea, Geneva tried her best to emulate it. She pushed against the water with the oars until she was far out enough to barely see the shore in the distance.

The cabinet made a loud splash as it plunged into the water, splashing saltwater back up onto the boat. Geneva grimaced and wiped her hands on her jeans.

Now, Luke was done with Holly forever.

***

Since her delicious meal, Geneva had never been in a better mood. At work, she was a little kinder with her patients. When her thoughts drifted to Luke, they were only happy musings. She wondered if he would like the dress she planned on wearing when she happened to run into him at his dermatologist appointment next week.

With his schedule handy, her mind was more at ease. She liked knowing where he was, not having to worry about what he was doing. It gave her time to plan out her next moves without anxiety.

She knew Holly's disappearance had been a bit of a burden on him. He reached out to her on social media after Geneva had sent the text from her phone. He was desperate to get into contact with Holly again, wondering if he had done something wrong.

Unfortunately for Holly, *she* had done something wrong by interfering with Geneva's plans. Soon, Luke would be back under Geneva's thumb again.

***

On the night Holly was supposed to star in her play, the news reported her mysteriously absent with many suspecting that she had run away. She disappeared from her small apartment with half-packed baggage left behind. With Luke's text confirming it, he was knew it was hopeless when he knocked on her door for hours with no reply. Geneva had watched him from the shadows, surprised and annoyed by the pain on his face, wondering why he didn't just move on and let her go already.

She would have given anything to take that pain away from him, but she knew it didn't work that way. This was her fault. She had done this to him. Geneva felt a smidgen of remorse for what she had done, but she knew that once Luke understood how perfect they were for each other, he would forgive her.

So now, all Geneva had to do was be at the right place at the right time.

***

The morning of his dermatologist appointment, she woke up and got dressed for the facial appointment she had made that overlapped with his.

She dressed in a navy-blue strapless dress. It hugged her curves without being overly tight and would make it seem like she had just come from work. Secretly, she had taken the whole day off for this escapade, hoping to create an opportunity to spend the day with Luke. If he was grieving, she was more than willing to be the shoulder he could cry on.

When she arrived at the dermatologist's office, Luke was already in the waiting room. He sat with a sports magazine open on his lap, tapping his fingers against the arm of the chair. There was no one else in the small waiting room, so when she made her entrance, he looked up at her and had no choice but to acknowledge her.

"What are you doing here?" he asked, his voice suspicious. Geneva could see that his eyes were red-rimmed and glassy. According to his schedule, he was here for a mole on the back of his neck he wanted to get checked out. He was dressed in a loose t-shirt and athletic shorts, a stark contrast from how he usually dressed.

"I have an appointment," she replied casually, a little miffed that he had given her the cold shoulder for so long. "Why are you dressed like Adam Sandler?"

Luke glanced down at his clothes and then back up at Geneva's face. "I've been stressed and busy, Geneva," he said glumly. "There's a lot going on right now."

Geneva murmured in understanding and then turned her back on him to check in at the receptionist's desk. He could deal with a little taste of his own medicine for a while. The woman behind the counter gave her a clipboard to fill out, so she carried it across the room and sat down beside Luke to fill out her paperwork.

"Why are you really here, Geneva?" he demanded, crossing his arms over his chest.

"I'm here for an appointment," she repeated.

"You have a knack for showing up wherever I am," Luke mused, sounding a little unsettled.

Geneva didn't want him to be afraid of her, so she tucked the clipboard against her chest and turned to look at him.

"I'm not following you, if that's what you're thinking," she said, maintaining direct eye contact with him in an exhilarating way. "And I don't believe in fate or anything like that. Surely, it isn't *that* crazy that we would bump into each other in this small town."

Luke let out a sigh. He said nothing, but he rubbed the sweaty palms of his hands against his shorts, his breath coming in quick pants. For some reason, he seemed really upset. To give him reprieve, Geneva walked back up to the reception desk and handed over her clipboard. When she returned to the waiting area, she sat across from him instead of beside him.

He was frightened prey, and she had to use her magnetic allure to set him back on the right track. She lowered her lashes and met his gaze.

"Thank you for referring that patient to me, by the way," she said demurely. "I haven't met with him yet, but I've got an appointment with him next week. It'll be nice to have someone new on the roster."

"Oh," Luke said, some of the tension draining from his shoulders. "Yeah, he's an awesome guy. Really funny and likeable. You'll enjoy the sessions, I'm sure."

"I'm sure," Geneva echoed.

A more comfortable silence settled between them. Though there was no one else in the waiting room with them, it seemed that the doctors were busy behind their closed doors. With her attuned senses, Geneva could hear a heated discussion going on in the back.

"Geneva?"

"Yes?"

"Do you want to go out and get some coffee after this?" he asked, his eyes guarded and grey. There was a pained reluctance lurking beneath his eyes, like he was forcing himself to ask her out for the sake of moving on. Geneva hated that he wasn't eager for her so much as he was desperately lonely.

Still, she could at least cure his loneliness.

"I'd love to," she said. "But you might have to wait on me. I don't know how long my session will take."

He looked up at her face, his eyes glimmering. "Facial?" he asked.

"How did you know?"

"I can tell by your skin," he said. "No woman your age has skin like that. You've been drinking the nectar of the gods or some shit."

Geneva laughed. "Something like that." She felt herself blushing, pleased that he noticed something pretty about her.

The doctor came into the room from the back, interrupting the intimate moment. Geneva tore her eyes away from him long enough to glare at the pretty doctor who called Luke's name as she stepped into the waiting room.

Obligingly, Luke stood up and followed her into the back. He gave Geneva a charming wink over his shoulder before he disappeared behind the door, but it did little to ease Geneva's mind. She hated the thought of him back there alone with that beautiful doctor. There was something dangerous about a woman with beauty *and* brains.

A moment later, another pretty doctor came out to call Geneva back for her facial. It was a procedure she had been through many times before, though there wasn't as much a need for it now that she was a vampire. She never aged, but that didn't mean she wasn't still prone to dry skin every now and then.

She had also been to this facility many times before for sun poisoning on her skin. Before she had adapted to the vampire world, the sun had been her biggest hurdle. She still underestimated the amount of sunscreen she needed sometimes since the amount she really needed seemed to leave her feeling encased in goo.

It was a necessary evil with the unintended side effect of keeping her looking young beyond even her vampiric years.

The experience was relaxing, especially since she could hear Luke and his doctor in the room that shared a wall with hers. While she enjoyed her facial massage, she listened to Luke complain about the mole he wanted removed from his neck.

Geneva found it entertaining that the doctor seemed to think the mole was aesthetically pleasing and had no problem telling Luke that. For some reason, it made Luke angry, a point of self-consciousness perhaps.

In the end, they agreed that since it was benign, they would leave it alone. Luke only agreed to this once he saw the estimate for the mole removal, another fact that Geneva found humorous.

By the time she walked back out into the lobby, she could see Luke waiting for her by the door. He wore a tight-lipped smile and seemed to be trying his best not to be in a bad mood. She decided it was probably best not to mention his mole today.

"Meat & Greet again?" she asked as she neared him.

"Yes, I love that place," Luke said with relief. "Everyone who works there is so nice. Plus, their burgers are the best I've had in years."

"Right," Geneva murmured, wondering if he had some kind of thing for one of the baristas or cashiers that worked there.

She walked close to him as they made their way to the restaurant, not too far a walk from the doctor's office.

She let her arm brush against his, delighting in the feeling of his warm skin against her. She imagined what it would feel like to be wrapped up in his arms, to receive texts from him like the ones he had sent to Holly.

"I'm sorry I haven't called," Luke apologized. "I wasn't exactly trying to ghost you."

"You weren't?" Geneva asked with a raised brow. She knew he had every intention of leaving her in the dust had things worked out with Holly. They were only together right now because of her work behind the scenes, and he wasn't even aware.

"I meant to tell you that I had started seeing someone else," he said, reluctant to meet her gaze.

The sun was high overhead and warm, beating down on Geneva in her dark dress. She felt herself sweating in the harsh rays.

"Things didn't work out?" she asked with her most sincere voice.

Luke shook his head. "I'm not sure where I went wrong."

They came to the door. Luke held it open for her, and Geneva walked inside. She gave him a sympathetic look as she passed beneath his arm, their faces scant inches from each other.

"I'm sure you didn't do anything wrong," she assured him. "You're perfect. If she couldn't see that, it's her fault. Not yours."

The corners of Luke's mouth tilted up into a hesitant grin. There was a small crack in the armor now. She just needed to hit a little harder.

When they got to the counter, there was a familiar face standing behind it. Michael waited with a smile to take their order, his gaze flicking between Geneva and Luke.

"Geneva," Michael said. "It's good to see you. A tea with cream and two sugars for you, and what can I get for your friend?"

"Black coffee, please," Luke said, pulling his wallet out from his back pocket. He handed Michael a twenty and then shoved the rest of the change into the tip jar. "Do you two know each other?" he asked Michael.

Michael busied himself with preparing their drinks, but he spared a moment to flash a beaming smile in Geneva's direction.

"She's a friend," Michael replied. "Bit of a regular here."

"I see," Luke said, giving Geneva a teasing glance, his lips curled into a wicked grin.

Geneva felt her face growing hotter by the second. She couldn't explain why, but she didn't want Michael and Luke to be anywhere near each other.

When Michael finally handed them both of their drinks, Geneva quickly found a table for them to sit down at. Instead of her usual corner table, Geneva found one near the window so she could look up at the sky. She chose the seat in the shade so she could see Luke's face illuminated by the sunlight.

He slid into the chair across from her, gripping his coffee cup tightly. He set it down on the table with a sharp *clop* and fixed her with a narrowed, scrutinizing look.

"Tell me, Geneva, because you're the expert," he began. "Do you think we would make a good couple?"

Caught off guard by the question, Geneva blinked at him. He blinked back at her, his eyes a swirling storm of clouds. Framed by his dark lashes, they were mesmerizing. She leaned a little closer, resting her elbows on the table.

"A perfect couple," she insisted. "Don't you agree? We're both of equal intelligence and attractiveness. Both driven and successful. We balance each other out in other ways. You're calm and collected whereas I can be brash and reactive. I think we'd be really great together if we ever got that chance."

Luke's smile faltered. It was clear he didn't quite know what to make of that.

"Maybe you're right," he finally said, his gaze drifting to the sidewalk just beyond the window.

There was a small gathering of pedestrians across the street, one of them a lithe blonde woman. Geneva couldn't help but notice his gaze on her.

"Is it because I'm not your type?" she asked.

"What?" he asked with a blink.

"You were going to ghost me because I'm not your type."

Luke refocused his gaze on her, admiring her and appreciating her beauty. She may not be blonde or petite, but Geneva knew she was pretty, and she knew Luke thought so too. She could see it in his eyes.

"You *are* my type, babe," he said earnestly, though Geneva wasn't sure she believed that. "Pretty women are always my type."

Geneva narrowed her eyes at him. He was worthless to her if he had a wandering eye. She wanted him as obsessed with her as she was with him. From the corner of her eye, she caught sight of Michael behind the counter, taking an order from a young girl in pigtails. She couldn't even keep Michael obsessed with her, let alone Luke.

"Listen," Luke said, seeing the look on her face. "I'm sorry for being kind of tepid with you. Actually, talking to that patient I was telling you about sort of helped me figure some things out. I know you might be upset with me, but I'd like to give this a serious shot."

The room seemed to stop spinning. Geneva's heart pounded against her ribcage. She couldn't believe what she was hearing. Her plan had worked even better than she had expected.

"Why with me?" she prodded. "Why not with someone young and blonde?" She nodded her head to the woman still standing across the street.

Luke had the decency to look ashamed. He glanced at the woman and let out a weary sigh. Geneva could see the absolute exhaustion behind his eyes.

"You have a compelling quality, Geneva," Luke said. "There's just something very intriguing about you. I won't lie. At first, I thought you were kind of creepy. But I think that's just how you are. You're very intense. I want to understand you better."

Geneva laughed. "As in therapy?" she teased. "Isn't that what sent your last girlfriend running for the hills?"

Luke recoiled, his brow furrowing as if he had just now considered this. He looked down into his cup of coffee, tapping the lip with the pad of his finger. Geneva watched him, feeling a stab of pity.

She wondered how much worse he would feel if he knew the truth about Holly.

"I'm sorry, Luke. Was that insensitive of me?"

He shook his head, dispelling whatever emotion was lurking behind his eyes.

"No, you're right," he said, plastering a fake smile on his face. "I have a tendency to overanalyze my partners and inadvertently push them away. I'd like to start over."

"Start over?" she asked.

"I wasn't fair to you from the beginning," he explained, and then took a long swig of coffee. He avoided her gaze for a moment, but his eyes were serious and focused when they finally found hers.

"I thought you were kind of weird," he admitted, his voice low. "When I found you on the pier that day, during the storm… Something about you just seemed strange. Your eyes were almost glowing, and you were, well, perfect. So beautiful I couldn't find a single flaw in you. I know I joked about it then, but I really believed you were a siren. I don't usually believe in the myths and legends of the sea, but when I saw you, I knew you couldn't be anything else."

Sweat dripped down the back of Geneva's neck. For him to suspect her of being a mythological creature might put her at risk, but at the same time, she loved that he had caught on to her mystique. She knew the allure the supernatural had on humans.

"That's a little cheesy, don't you think?" she teased.

"I'm being serious," Luke insisted. "You *are* a siren, aren't you? Why do you seem so perfect? What else could it be?"

Geneva rolled her eyes.

"Luke, if I were a siren, that would mean I'd be trying to lure you to your death," she explained. "I don't want you to die. Besides, you haven't heard me sing. I promise you that hearing me sing in the car would prove to you that I'm not a siren."

He gave her a skeptical look, crossing his arms over his chest.

"There's something fishy about you, Geneva," he said. "I'm going to find out what it is."

"Is that your way of asking me on another date?" she asked.

Luke cracked a smile at her and then laughed.

"You know what?" he said. "Yes. Yes, it is."

***

Luke forgot about Holly in no time. After reconnecting at the dermatologist's office, Geneva and Luke started hanging out more often. He was kinder to her this time around, less teasing and flirtatious, kinder and more curious.

She suggested they go to the aquarium for their next date, an idea that Luke was delighted to take her up on. They had a pleasant day walking around in the dark, their fingers twisted together while he told her nerdy facts about the fish.

Afterwards, they went to dinner at Carmello's, stuffed themselves with breadsticks and tiramisu, and by the time the night had drawn to an end, they still wanted more of each other.

***

Over the next few weeks, they consistently met up after work to hang out at the coffee corner. Sometimes, Luke brought a book to read, or Geneva brought some patient files to review. It was nice to just be in each other's company.

But it felt strange to do so under the watchful eye of Michael, though to Geneva's disappointment, he seemed content to see her together with Luke. She had expected him to at least be a little bothered, but he almost seemed like he was happy for her.

She could tell by the saccharine scent of Michael's blood that he was attracted to her, so she didn't understand why he wasn't jealous. She was annoyed that it bothered her so much, especially now that she had Luke in her clutches again.

Luke, on the other hand, did seem a little irritated by her preoccupation with Michael. She was not so keen on hiding the direction of her gaze, and when Luke eventually caught on to who she was looking at, he snapped his fingers to bring her focus back to him.

"That guy is your friend, right?" he asked.

Geneva nodded.

"Why do you keep staring at him?"

She smiled at Luke and reached out to lace their fingers together. "Luke, I only have eyes for you, if that's what you're getting at," she said softly. "I'm just worried about him, that's all."

Luke shifted in his seat, a puppyish look of eagerness coming to his features. "Why are you worried about him?" he pressed, his psychologist instincts kicking in.

Geneva gave him a scathing but still amused look.

"He hasn't been acting like himself," she explained. "He's hiding his emotions."

Luke looked over at Michael and watched him flitting around behind the counter, preparing drinks and taking orders. His face was mostly obscured by the blue visor he wore, but they could both see that his mouth was set in a grim line.

"You think something's bothering him?" Luke asked.

Geneva shook her head and then flicked her gaze back to Luke. "I don't want to talk about him," she said, rubbing her thumb over his hand. Their affection had taken a more physical turn lately. Whenever they were near each other, they always seemed to be holding hands or leaning into one another.

It made Geneva's thirst pound in her veins. She exerted monumental effort to keep her fangs at bay whenever he would kiss her.

Other than that, Geneva had no complaints. Life was easy with Luke by her side. She always had a date for when she wanted to see a movie. Her sister was finally off her back about her relationship woes. Luke seemed to get along well with Eugenia, but not so well that Geneva found it in herself to be jealous.

She knew her sister would never do that to her, but the instinct to be jealous was still there. Geneva never stopped struggling to think that every woman around them was trying to steal Luke from her.

But once Luke got over his initial fear and hesitation, it was easy to make him fall in love with her. Geneva's compelling vampiric beauty and lurid seduction of him left him begging for more. Just one night together had been enough to get him firmly lodged under her thumb. To keep him there would be easy.

At work, she no longer had him constantly on her mind. She was more at ease to focus on her responsibilities, especially since she could still check his schedule at any given time to see what he was up to.

The patient he had referred to her came in for his appointment, a stout, surly man with a thick mustache and an even thicker personality.

"Name's Baxter," he said sharply, sliding onto the couch opposite Geneva's desk. "I'm only here because Luke promised me you can fix all my problems."

"I doubt that's what Luke promised you," Geneva replied, tapping her pencil against her mouth. Already, she was beginning to suspect something fishy about this referral.

"He told me you could get my wife off my back," he countered. "Can you do that?"

Geneva frowned at him and crossed her arms over her chest.

"Baxter, why are you really here?" she asked. "What did you want from Luke, and what do you want from me?"

"I don't feel emotionally connected to my wife," he replied. "Or anyone, really. I love her. Or I guess I do. I really just want her to leave me alone."

Silence settled over the room, except for the ticking clock on the wall. Geneva watched him for a moment, trying to better understand why Luke had sent him to her.

"You don't want to feel emotionally connected to your own wife?" Geneva pressed.

"Oh, I *want* to," Baxter answered. "I'm just not sure that I'm capable of it. Maybe I'm a sociopath or something. I thought that's what you're supposed to figure out."

Geneva ignored the jab, wondering if this was Luke's way of trying to figure out how to connect with her emotionally. There was undeniably a wall still between them, one entirely of Geneva's doing. Her vampirism and murdering and manipulating were always going to be a barrier between them. As long as Luke never realized it was there, it wasn't a problem.

But sending her a message like this through a patient was a sign that he knew there was some kind of wall keeping them apart. He believed it to be a lack of emotional connection, and that was something she could easily remedy.

"Hello? Are you listening to me?"

Geneva whipped her gaze back to Baxter, who was flushed with anger, his mustache bristling with his boar-like breath.

"I'm listening," Geneva insisted. "Go on."

"What should I do about my wife?" he asked.

"You should ask yourself why you're with her," Geneva instructed. "Why do you love her, and why does she love you?"

Baxter opened his mouth to reply, but then shut it again, speechless.

"You can think about it until our next session," Geneva said, standing up to get the door for him. Begrudging he stood up, a little disgruntled that she was ending their session so abruptly and allowed her to usher him back into the lobby. Geneva slammed her office door shut behind him without so much as a goodbye or a second thought.

She returned to her desk and sat down with a sigh, wondering how she could convince Luke that there was no wall between them. He wanted to feel emotionally connected to her, and the best way to do that was to tell him that she loved him.

Geneva had known in her heart for a long time that she loved Luke, or would at least come to love him. She realized it when she first laid eyes on him at the pier, though it hadn't occurred to her until just now. It had been something wild and sub-conscious, something deep in the roots of her soul that led her to Luke, her soulmate.

So, when he invited her over to his house the next night, Geneva was eager to go and share her feelings with him.

She went straight to his house after work, wondering how a man with an empty refrigerator could cook her a meal as grand as the one he had promised her. When she arrived at his house, the kitchen smelled of roasted tomato and basil.

"Homemade pizza?" she asked when he opened the oven and removed the brick plate on which sat two personal-sized pizzas with a rugged, homemade quality to them.

"I was getting tired of fish," he said with a chuckle. "I thought I'd try something a little different. I ate a lot of pizza at the bowling alley growing up. It's sort of nostalgic for me. And who doesn't like pizza?"

Geneva smiled at him, charmed by the innocent memory. She wondered if perhaps the bowling alley was still a prevalent part of his life because he was still trying to cling to his childhood. That meant that no matter how disgusted she was by his love for the bowling alley, she couldn't tease him for it. He would become defensive and guarded again.

"I always liked pizza," Geneva replied, glad that they at least had that in common. "My sister and I used to order it every Monday when we watched The Bachelor."

Luke wrinkled his nose in disgust. "You're actually into shows like that?" he asked incredulously. "I thought you were above that kind of mindless television."

"It's a guilty pleasure," she said defensively. "Is that not what fishing and bowling are for you?"

"Fishing and bowling require *skill*," he explained.

"Bowling doesn't require *that* much skill," she defended.

Luke grinned wolfishly at her in a way that made butterflies flurry up in her stomach. He stood at the stove, cutting the pizzas into more manageable slices. When he was finished, he joined Geneva at the table, sitting down on the chair across from her.

It felt weirdly domestic to be enjoying dinner with him in his house. She could imagine eating dinner here for the rest of her life, spending her evenings in Luke's company every day after work, forging a life together with him.

His mood seemed to have vastly improved since Holly's disappearance, much to Geneva's relief. It felt nice to have his attention on her again.

"I'm having a good time with you, Geneva," he said after taking a bit of his pizza. "I think maybe our relationship is fated. You told me you didn't believe in that kind of thing."

Geneva didn't, but she would pretend to believe anything for Luke.

"I do," she lied. "At least, now I do. I agree that people are put into your life for a reason sometimes."

Luke nodded. "Sometimes, it feels like life is pushing me toward you," he explained. "I tried to resist it at first, but I think there may be a higher power leading us toward each other."

Inwardly, Geneva winced, feeling a stab of guilt. She did not believe in a higher power. The only thing guiding them toward each other was her. But his train of thought was beneficial for her, no matter how silly she thought it was.

"You mean God?" she pressed.

Luke shrugged. "I don't know about that," he said. "I think you know what I mean, though. The way we keep finding each other… it seems supernatural."

Geneva laughed, but her chuckles faded quickly when Luke glared at her.

"I'm serious," he said. "You may think it's nonsense, but I believe it."

She gave him a patronizing look. "Well, that seems like a pretty big swing in the opposite direction from ghosting me," she said. "How do I know you aren't just leading me on again so you can toy with me?"

Luke gave her a hurt look and dropped his pizza back onto the plate.

"I wasn't trying to lead you on," he said, his voice wrought with guilt. "It wasn't my intention to toy with you, either. I would never do something like that. I hope you know that you can trust me. If the way I went about discovering my feelings for you hurt you, I'm so sorry. Romance isn't always easy to navigate."

"Especially not for us psychologists," she replied, giving him a wary glance.

He let out a bitter chuckle.

"You believe me, though, don't you?" he pressed. "I would *never* do anything to intentionally hurt you. It's important to me that you understand that."

"I understand," Geneva said, though truthfully, she wasn't sure she believed him. She knew he would turn on her in a heartbeat if he realized all the atrocities she had committed over the years.

It seemed like he was actually getting serious about their relationship now, that she wasn't just some charming flirt to him anymore. She was grateful that he was getting serious, but it opened a whole new slew of problems for her, problems she would have to work out, now under his watchful eye.

If he was serious, that meant she needed to act quickly, send their relationship into overdrive. She couldn't afford to wait to lock him into marriage. He was a young, attractive, charming man. Any woman like Holly could snatch him away from her at any moment. She would only be safe once she had his ring on her finger.

So, her next task on the agenda was to find a way to make him propose.

Chapter Twelve

Despite Geneva's best efforts, the police opened an investigation into Holly's disappearance. Of course, they hadn't found a body yet, but they already suspected foul play. After her family had hired a private investigator to find out where she had gone, they found evidence of a forced entry, causing Geneva to begin to panic.

As long as she kept a low profile and didn't feed again for a while (or at least didn't kill anyone in the process), she would be fine.

Unfortunately, her thirst grew unbearable after just a short time with no human blood in her system. Each time she fed, the fiery thirst grew stronger.

Combined with her close proximity to Luke, her fangs were almost always out, forcing her to be careful about opening her mouth until she had forced them to recede. Perhaps she was overly cautious, but she had taken to carrying around a set of fake, costume vampire teeth in her purse in case anyone saw. At least it was a somewhat reasonable excuse if she had proof, even if it was silly.

Despite the fear of incrimination, it was still worth it to spend that blissful time with Luke. He took her on romantic dates, pulling out all his charms and tricks to woo her. She didn't really need wooing; she was already head-over-heels for him.

He was relentlessly happy to be around her and excited to be properly dating someone. It was clear he hadn't had a serious girlfriend in a while. Geneva suspected he had been planning to ask Holly to be his girlfriend, so it wasn't exactly a shock to her when he asked her instead.

He went all out, taking her to the ballet to see a show, even though it was clearly out of his element. Afterward, they went to dinner, and then a romantic walk through the small town's botanical garden. It was the perfect evening, and when he asked Geneva to be his girlfriend underneath the silvery moonlight, it was the perfect end to a perfect date.

Of course, she agreed, more than eager to become a legitimate couple. From there, a marriage proposal would be a piece of cake.

They fell easily into life as a couple, despite their rough beginnings. Luke was a sweet boyfriend, always sending her flowers at work and cooking dinner for her. He was always tender and reverent when he touched her, not hungry and possessive like most men were. It was a refreshing change of pace, but it just cemented the fact that he thought she was worthy of his affection because of whatever supernatural reason he suspected.

It made her have doubts about whether or not Luke *truly* wanted her, or if he was only enamored by the idea of a siren lover. Regardless, she had done enough to manipulate his feelings that, even without that factor, she still doubted.

Though it unsettled Geneva, there was nothing that could be done about it. Things were going so well with him that she wasn't inclined to do anything to ruin that.

Not long after they began dating, Luke asked Geneva to move in with him. She thought it was a little soon for a man to be asking her that, but she was thrilled anyway. She eagerly agreed, ready to permanently stake her claim on him.

The first time she slept in his bed beside him, she felt the first sense of belonging that she deserved. It was nice to be pressed against his side, to fall asleep nestled beneath his arm. She had never known a feeling like that before, though she had spent the night with many men in her life.

Luke was something special, and she had to keep him close. Luckily for her, he was completely captivated with her. She could tell by the way he looked at her, and more succinctly, by the smell of his blood. Affection and adoration had made it unbearably sweet. It became harder to resist his blood the closer they got.

***

One night, he crawled into bed after he had nicked himself shaving. She tasted the blood on his cheek when she kissed him and was forced to flee the room. She slept on the couch that night, though she couldn't properly explain to him why. She told him she just needed a little space, and he had seemed understanding.

She had no one to complain about that experience to, which always made her feel like she was alone in this. Many times, she wished she had a vampire friend she could explain these things to. The only person she could think of who would take her vampirism in stride was Michael.

She had played with the idea of telling Michael what a monster she really was, but in the back of her mind, she worried that he would become afraid of her. She couldn't bear to lose one of her only friends, not for something that was out of her control.

Unfortunately, telling Luke was entirely too risky. She was afraid he wouldn't be as understanding as Michael, nor would he want to be with her anymore once he realized all the things her vampirism had led her to do. He was smart. He would see what she had done to manipulate him if the truth ever came out. He could never know about Holly, about breaking into his house, craving his blood. He would never trust her again.

But Geneva couldn't keep those feelings bottled inside anymore. She had to tell someone what she was feeling. If only there were therapists for vampires. There had never been any rule book, and she still struggled with her bloodlust and aggression even after a couple years.

And Michael was the least aggressive person she knew. Perhaps, he might have some practical advice for her. And if he turned against her, she could always kill him. She was hesitant to do something like that, but at least, he would make a tasty snack.

So, one day after work, instead of heading home to Luke, Geneva went to see Michael. It was strange to be back on her old routine after so long. She had stopped coming to the restaurant so often once she moved in with Luke. When she walked in and smelled the strong, lingering scent of coffee beans and burgers, she realized how much she had missed it.

She walked up to the counter where Michael was cleaning the espresso machine with a white cloth. He glanced up at her, and a smile drifted lazily to his face.

"Geneva," he said with delight. "Long time no see. I thought you had forgotten about me."

She gave him a weak smile.

"Listen, Michael, I want to talk to you about something serious," she explained. "Do you have time to get a drink with me later? After work?"

Michael's brow furrowed with confusion.

"It must be something bad," he said warily.

"No, no," she gushed. "It's not bad. Well, I don't think it is. But it's definitely a conversation we can't have here."

He gave her a skeptical look.

"I get off in an hour," he said. "Can you hang out here until then?"

Geneva nodded and ordered a black tea with cream and sugar. She found her seat in the corner and passed the time on her phone, looking through some of the photos she had taken of her and Luke on some of their dates.

She eavesdropped on several conversations and was surprised to feel a stab of jealousy when she overheard two teenage girls talking about the cute barista who made their drinks with extra whipped cream on top. Geneva wasn't sure why she felt the sudden acerbic swell of anger at them, but for some reason, it extended to Michael, too.

When he was finally finished with his shift and came to her table, his expression was a mixture of curiosity and contentedness. It seemed he wasn't worried about whatever she had to say to him, which was a good thing, but it also sort of made her concerned.

She crossed her arms over her chest as he approached, watching the girls behind him snicker and giggle as he passed. She got up to her feet and slung her purse over her shoulder, giving Michael a scathing look as she stepped out onto the street.

Michael chased after her, his face scrunched in bewilderment.

"Are you mad at me?" he demanded. "What's with the attitude?"

"I'm not mad at you," she said coldly. "I just feel bad for those poor adolescent girls in there you flirted with. You know they're too young for you, right?"

Shocked, Michael recoiled and blinked at her.

"I wasn't flirting with them," he said defensively.

Geneva narrowed her eyes at him. She wanted to present him with the extra whipped cream evidence, but it didn't seem like a good idea to start up an argument about it right now. He would only think she was being petty.

"Fine, whatever," Geneva said dismissively, and she coldly turned her shoulder on him to continue walking down the street.

Michael followed after her in silence. She could feel his unrelenting, piercing gaze on her back the entire walk to the bar. His blood was ripe and sour, not exactly a good sign given what she was about to tell him. She had to admit to herself, though, that she was curious about what his blood would smell like after this conversation.

When they were finally seated at the bar, each with a beer in hand, Michael turned and looked at Geneva expectantly.

"Well? What did you want to talk to me about?"

Geneva took a long swig of her beer and then took a deep breath. Her palms were sweating just thinking about confessing her secret. She had never told anyone before, afraid of what would happen to her if word got out.

But she had to trust Michael. There was no one else she could trust.

"What I'm about to tell you is a secret, okay?" she explained, meeting his gaze with serious eyes. "You can't tell a soul about this. Promise me."

"I promise," Michael said quickly, his eyes eager and alert now.

"It's going to sound really strange and almost unbelievable, but I need you to believe me," she begged. "Please, just hear me out, and I'll explain everything."

Michael's expression grew worried. "You haven't even told me what it is yet."

Geneva swallowed. "I'm a vampire," she blurted, holding his gaze despite the overwhelming urge to look away from the strange murkiness of his eyes.

It was clear he didn't know what to think. His brow twitched, and the corner of his mouth melded into an unreadable half-smile, half-frown.

"A vampire?" he asked, his tone neutral.

Geneva struggled to hold back her tears as she nodded. It was a relief to get it off her chest, even if she wasn't quite sure of Michael's reaction yet.

"So… um, how did that happen?" Michael asked, rubbing the back of his neck.

He was struggling to take her seriously, but she appreciated that he was at least making an effort.

Hesitantly, she glanced around the bar and made sure no one was looking before she slid aside the collar of her dress and exposed the two fang marks on her neck.

"I thought that was a mole," Michael mused, leaning closer to get a good look. It was more like a scar than a mole, but still no concrete evidence of her vampirism.

"I was bitten," she explained, straightening her collar. "It was several years ago on a first date. We had a fun, kinky night. He bit me, and we fell asleep. Never saw him again. But after that, I started feeling strange."

Michael's expression shifted again. He rested one elbow on the bar and leaned a little closer, waiting to hear what she would say next.

So, Geneva unloaded everything on him. She explained her first battles with bloodlust, her first kill. She described how it felt to drink blood, the way her veins strung with pain without it in her system. She wasn't a bad person. She didn't *want* to kill. Except she enjoyed it. She liked the scent of fear, the tang of cowering blood.

Michael listened attentively to every word she said, silent as stone on his barstool across from her. He nodded along as she spoke, and the words just kept flowing. She couldn't control them.

She spilled everything. Stalking Luke, killing Holly. All of the things she had kept bottled inside spewed out of her and right into Michael, who seemed to be taking it all in stride.

As a psychologist herself, she understood why it was good, and even necessary, for her mental health to get these things off her chest. She was also aware of what an irresponsible burden she had now put on Michael.

His blood reeked of anxiety, not fear, but something adjacent to it.

"That's a lot to take in, Geneva," he said, his breath a little shaky.

They shared a meaningful glance between them. She was sure that Michael could see the turmoil on her face, which wasn't something she usually let show. In this case, she couldn't really help it, but at least, it seemed to make Michael more inclined to believe her.

For a moment, neither of them knew what to say. A terse silence settled between them. Geneva swallowed, trying to squash down the feeling of anxiety buzzing in her ribcage. She hadn't consumed any blood since she killed Holly, and the thirst was starting to get to her.

"Why are you telling me this?" Michael asked. "Why not tell Luke instead? Or does he know, too?"

"No," Geneva said with a shake of her head. "He doesn't know. You're the only person I've told. I can't tell Luke for obvious reasons."

"But you trust *me*?" he pressed.

He was giving her such an intensely curious, and somewhat angry, look that Geneva let her mouth fall shut, not knowing what to say.

"I thought you would be the one person I could trust. You've always listened to what I've had to say before, even if you didn't like it," she finally said, her voice cautious and careful. Michael's bitterness was unexpected, but she knew him well enough to know that he was still a kind person deep down. He wouldn't abandon her for something like this. But understandably, he still wanted answers.

Michael's expression softened. He reached his hand across the counter and wrapped it around hers, his eyes warm but serious.

"You can trust me, Geneva," he said softly. "I'm not going to tell anyone your secret. But you do know that you need help, right? You're obviously not in great control of yourself. People have died because of your indiscretions. You don't want that happening again, do you?"

Geneva sighed and then gave an indifferent shrug. "I don't *want* to kill people," she conceded, "but I need to drink blood to survive. Without it, sunscreen isn't enough to keep me walking in the sunlight. It's painful; the withdrawals are excruciating. I'll die without blood."

Michael gave her a sympathetic look. Geneva could tell that he was still rattled, and she admired his dedication to helping her.

"What about blood banks?" he suggested. "Maybe you can get a supply without having to kill anyone in the process."

She blinked. That wasn't something she had considered before, mostly because of the appeal of the kill, the added factor of warm blood pumping through fearful, rushing veins. It was far more satisfying than a Capri Sun blood bag, though of course, she didn't know that for sure. How would it even taste good if it was cold?

"You don't like that idea?" Michael ventured.

"It's something to consider," she said vaguely, not wanting to get into that issue with him right now when he still seemed a little freaked out.

"Listen, Geneva, I'm glad you told me," he said. "I'm glad you know you can trust me. You can, I promise. I want to help you, even if I don't know how yet."

Geneva let out a bitter laugh. "I'm probably beyond help," she explained. "There isn't really an instruction guide on how to do this."

"No, I suppose not," Michael murmured. "Still, I want to try my best to help you. Next time you feel that uncontrollable bloodlust, call me. I'll see if I can talk you down."

"Seriously?" she asked incredulously.

"Yeah," he scoffed. "I don't mean to brag, but I'm pretty good at that kind of thing."

"I believe that," Geneva laughed. "This is a little different, though. You've never talked anyone out of draining someone's blood, I bet."

"No," he agreed, "but you should at least let me try. You don't have anything to lose."

Geneva wasn't so sure that was true. She could lose Luke from this, if not from her vampirism, but from her close relationship with Michael. She knew that she wouldn't appreciate Luke leaning on another woman for help with something so big. It was just one more thing she would have to hide from him.

"Well, the thing is," she continued awkwardly. "The bloodlust is always at its worse when I'm feeling... regular lust."

A blush came to his cheeks, which in turn, made his blood sharp and pungent in the air. It wasn't strong enough to activate her fangs, but it made her gums tingle, and her pulse quicken.

"I see."

"It happens a lot when I'm with Luke," she said, feeling a blush come to her own cheeks. "The other night, he cut himself shaving, and I had to leave the room. I'm worried that I might hurt him, but I really love Luke. I don't want anything bad to happen to him because of me."

Michael's mouth twisted into a frown. He let his gaze fall anywhere but on her, his cheeks still tinged with pink.

"What about animal blood?" he asked, his voice a little raspy. "Have you tried drinking that to curb the cravings?"

Geneva wrinkled her nose in distaste. She had never once considered drinking animal blood as it had a dirty, unappealing smell. Somewhere in her mind, she rationalized that animals had purer souls than people. Something about killing them felt more wrong than killing humans, but maybe that was just her vampirism talking.

"I guess cat blood wouldn't be so bad," she said, "but is it really any better to have a shed full of dead cats?"

Michael blinked at her. "You don't have a shed full of dead humans, do you?"

"No, of course not," she said to his obvious relief. "I always dispose of them properly."

He gave her an unreadable look and motioned for the bartender. Silence settled between them again, but it wasn't exactly uncomfortable. Michael ordered another beer and chugged almost half of it before he spoke again.

"I'm happy to help you, Geneva, but I think I need some time to process this."

He chugged the rest of his beer and then slammed the empty bottle on the counter. Geneva watched him wipe his mouth on his sleeve and then check his watch, dread forming in her stomach.

"You sure know how to keep a man on his toes."

She reached out and touched his hand the same way he had touched hers, forcing him to meet her gaze. Reluctantly, he looked into her eyes and swallowed a lump in his throat.

"Thank you, Michael," she said earnestly. "I know I'm asking a lot of you, but I knew you'd be willing to help. I appreciate it."

"No problem, Geneva," he said with a soft smile.

He reached into his pocket and pulled out a wad of bills that he placed on the counter beside his empty beer bottle. He gave her a quick, but somehow still affectionate, smile and then walked out of the bar. Geneva watched him, her stomach fluttering.

She wasn't really sure if that went well or not. Michael was good at hiding his emotions. The scent of his blood didn't lie, even if his words had been accepting and supportive. She glanced at the time on her phone and noticed how late it was getting.

Luke would be furious if she showed up late in the early hours of morning, drunk.

Instead of ordering another beer like she wanted to, Geneva went home. The lights were off when she walked through the front door. Luke was already in bed asleep when she wandered into the bedroom, which she was grateful for. She slipped into her pajamas and then climbed into bed and settled next to Luke.

As she laid her head on his chest, and his unconscious instinct brought him to settle his arm over her, she wondered if she were capable of going the rest of her life without killing anyone. Maybe she *could* survive on animal blood or a blood bank supply. Even now, she didn't feel the nudge of her fangs, though Luke's heartbeat was loud and steady in her ear. It was as if just getting the urges off her chest helped curb them in some way.

Whatever tension was between her and Michael was nothing more than a growing pain, a necessary one. If she wanted to marry Luke soon, she needed to figure out a way to control herself, and Michael was the only person she could trust with the job.

Chapter Thirteen

Geneva woke up the next morning wrapped in Luke's arms. His face was nuzzled into her hair, his body pressed warmly against her back. His thumb rubbed absently at her arm, and he let out a contented, comfortable sigh.

"Good morning," Geneva said with a grin, warm and happy.

"Good morning," he replied, a cheerful rasp in his voice. He arched his back and held her a little tighter, repositioning his chin on top of her head.

They stayed like that, a tangle of limbs and sheets, for a moment. The Sunday morning sunrise was visible through the bedroom window, cotton candy clouds floating across the pink sky. They watched together as the sky changed colors, enjoying the blissful moment of no stress or work or blood or anything else.

"Where were you last night?" Luke asked, shattering the serene bubble that had enveloped the room. His tone didn't sound accusatory, but Geneva immediately felt blushed and nervous anyway.

She shifted in his arms until she could see his face, and then she reached up to touch his cheek. It did bother her to have to lie to him. More lies meant more to keep up with. Eventually, that kind of thing would implode on her. She had to be careful about exactly *how much* she had to keep Luke in the dark.

"I just needed a little alone time," she said. "To recharge, you know? We've been living together almost a month now, and I love it, don't get me wrong. It's just that I've never lived with anyone before, and sometimes, it feels like too much."

Luke smiled at her, rubbing his palm up and down her arm. "Every couple needs time apart," he agreed. "You would know better than I do."

Geneva chuckled.

"I like living with you, too," Luke said, dropping a kiss on her forehead. "I especially like waking up with you like this."

She snuggled closer, settling her head in the crook of his neck and shoulder. His blood smelled incredibly sweet, but instead of feeling thirsty, she felt a swelling affection for Luke, who always managed to be so charming.

"I love you, Luke," she blurted, glad they couldn't see each other's face so he wouldn't notice the horrible heat in her cheeks.

To her delight, she felt the pulse in his neck quicken against her temple.

"I love you, too," Geneva," he murmured into her hair.

***

Geneva kept her charms up as her relationship with Luke progressed. Though she still felt violent urges of jealousy and lust, she had gotten better at controlling them. True to his word, Michael answered every phone call she ever made to him, all the times she felt compelled to snap and murder a waitress whose gaze lingered a little too long on Luke when they were at dinner, or to suck all the blood from Luke's body when they got a little too heated.

It was a fine balance to walk, but it was actually worked. She had taken Michael's advice and started stealing a supply of blood from a local blood bank. With her credentials, it was easy to convince them to donate a supply to her small town, especially since she was able to forge the documents for a fake charity she had created.

With a steady supply of blood, her urges weren't nearly as strong. It wasn't quite the same as drinking straight from the veins, but it was good enough to get her through the weeks.

Michael helped her through her turbulent emotions when the guilt started to overwhelm her. She had taken to venting all her troubles to him after work, resurfacing her old habit of going to Meat & Greet in the afternoons. Feelings that she had denied herself, bottled inside, now began to flow through her freely.

Unfortunately, she drove them straight into Michael. It came to a point where every conversation with him had her in tears or anger. He became a battering ram for all her feelings, which made her feel even more guilty. But without him, she wouldn't be able to have her relationship with Luke, and she wanted it so badly she was willing to let

Michael take the hit as long as it meant she could keep up her charade.

Especially since Luke planned to propose soon. Geneva found the receipt from a jeweler sent to his email, a substantial amount of money for a ring. They had never discussed marriage with each other before, but she knew from pillow-talk conversations with him that marriage was something that was important to him. He wanted to have a family and children one day, and well, he wasn't getting any younger.

She worried that as a vampire, she wouldn't be able to carry a human baby. She had no idea how that biology worked, but she supposed that was a bridge she'd have to cross when she came to it.

There was enough stress in her life as it was. She didn't need to be thinking about things like that now. She could worry about that stuff after Luke had proposed, after his ring was on her finger.

When Luke asked her if she wanted to go to Carmello's, Geneva knew the time had come. She put on her fanciest dress for the upscale restaurant, a deep red flared dress in a style she knew Luke liked, though it was certainly not her preference. She loved the way he looked at her when she wore dresses like that, so she was more than willing to sacrifice her style for his happiness, especially on a night like this one.

The restaurant was empty when they arrived, the tables all removed from the dining room except for one. The massive, ornately gilded dining room was filled with candles and soft string music. Geneva's cheeks hurt from smiling as Luke walked her over to the table and pulled out her chair for her to sit.

"You rented out the whole restaurant for me?" she asked in awe, gazing at the silk tablecloth and glimmering candles.

She could see the string quartet in the corner of the dimly lit room, and the swinging movements of their playing.

"Of course, I did, babe," Luke said as if it were nothing. "You're worth every penny. And now, I can have you all to myself."

Geneva smiled demurely at him, her heart fluttering in her chest. Luke sat down across from her, his eyes sparkling over the votive candles at the center of the table.

"What's the occasion?" she pressed.

Luke grinned embarrassedly at her and then glanced at the menus on the table between them.

"I wanted to wait until after dinner, but I think you already know what's coming," he said, reaching into his pocket. "Geneva, you are the brightest, prettiest, most charming woman I have ever met. I know we haven't been dating long, but I feel like we have an amazing connection. I know that you're the person I want to spend the rest of my life with, the person I want to start a family with. I love you more than I've loved anyone else."

With a pounding heart, Geneva leaned across the table and reached for his hand.

"I love you, too," she whispered across the table.

He pulled the ring box up to the table and flipped it open to reveal a large princess cut diamond inlaid in a gold band. The extravagance of it matched the price Geneva had seen on his receipt, but it still shocked her all the same. She could only imagine how much of his savings he had spent to buy her a ring like this, especially on his mediocre salary.

"I want you to be my wife, Geneva Beck," he said earnestly. "Will you marry me?"

"Yes," Geneva gushed before he even finished the sentence. "I'd love to be your wife, Luke Mason."

She extended her hand for the ring, and he slipped it onto her finger, his hands trembling and his breath shaky. His nervousness was charming, and Geneva couldn't help but grin at him.

"I was planning on getting down on one knee," he said, rubbing his thumb over the diamond as he held her hand. "I have something else planned, actually. It would have been super romantic to propose at the end of the date, but now, I'll get to do those things with my fiancé instead."

Geneva felt warm and tingly as she slipped her hand out of his grasp so she could put her elbows on the table, rest her chin on her hands, and stare at him. It was hard to believe that he was officially hers, this charming, handsome, intelligent man. The fact that he couldn't wait until the end of the date to propose was immensely satisfying.

"What else did you have planned?" she asked.

"You'll see, babe," he said. "I want it to be a surprise."

"Luke, you know I don't like surprises," she warned. She was shocked that he even had a surprise for her. She was usually so good at knowing what he was up to. She was already surprised that he had rented out the entire restaurant without her knowing.

It had her curiosity piqued.

They enjoyed a delicious lobster dinner together, reminiscing about when they first met and dreaming about the future. They talked about where they would live, whether they would ever want to work at the same office together. Though Geneva didn't want to raise the subject, they even talked about how many children they would have.

She pretended to be on the fence about it, but the truth was that she didn't want to have any children, not even one. She didn't even know if she *could* have any. The only way to confirm that would be by trying, but she didn't want to risk having a half-vampire baby. She couldn't possibly put a child through what she had been through over the last few years.

But if it made Luke happy, she would let him think that she might be persuaded into having a child one day. Adoption was still a possibility, even if her vampirism kept her from biologically being able to carry one.

The conversation was a much needed and intimate one, and after they shared a chocolate mousse dessert and left the restaurant, Geneva had never felt closer to Luke. She twined their fingers together as they walked down the street, her body pressed warmly against his side.

Her eyes kept drifting to the glinting diamond on her finger, her heart swelling with happiness every time.

"So, where are we going next?" she asked, peering up at him with admiration and affection.

"It's a bit of a drive from here," he explained. "About an hour. I promise it will be worth it, though. It'll give you a chance to listen to my terrible singing in the car."

Geneva laughed. "I've heard you sing in the shower. You're not bad."

He gave her a disarming grin. "Are *you*? I don't think I've ever heard you sing."

"I don't sing," she said. "I sound like a croaking frog when I do."

"We'll see about that."

She followed him into the parking garage, and he started up the car. They drove in silence for a little while, Geneva gazing at the stars through the window, her forehead pressed against the glass. The stars were thick in the sky overhead, mesmerizing in a way she couldn't take her eyes away from, not even for Luke.

Eventually, he turned on the radio. He sang old seventies tunes for her and even got her to sing along to a few. It was an easy co-existence inside that car, a feeling Geneva wished she could capture for eternity. She had never felt so happy.

Despite the fact that Luke had a surprise waiting for her, she was eager to spend the rest of the night with him and was not at all daunted by the fact that she had no idea where they were going.

Finally, Luke pulled off the main highway and onto a suspiciously rural exit. Geneva noticed the signs for a campground nearby and turned her wary gaze to Luke.

"We aren't going camping, are we?" she asked hesitantly.

He gave her a scathing look. "Of course not, babe. I know you better than that," he said teasingly. "If I were going to take you camping, I'd at least make sure you wore appropriate clothes."

She narrowed her gaze on him, unsure how the clothes she *was* wearing were appropriate for being out here in the mountainous woods.

"Trust me," he said, clasping his hand over her knee. "You'll love it."

Geneva fell silent as he pulled into a gravel parking lot and turned off the ignition. If she weren't a vampire, she would've been a little spooked to be out here in the woods at night. If there were any predators out here, Geneva would have to defend herself and let Luke see the true scope of her abilities. She didn't want that to happen, at least, not yet. The idea made her feel a little nervous.

"Don't worry, Geneva," Luke said, handing her a flashlight as they started walking down the dirt path through the trees. "I won't let anything happen to you."

Geneva refrained from laughing. She took Luke's hand as he dragged her down the path, her heart beating fast with anticipation. The trail wasn't very long, and when the trees began to part, Geneva could see a faint yellow glow on the horizon.

Curious, she quickened her pace until the trees cleared away to reveal a small lake filled with floating votives. The short pier had a little rowboat waiting for them, complete with a bottle of champagne and a plaid throw blanket.

"Luke…" Geneva said in awe, staring at the beautiful scene around her.

The lake was calm and silent aside from the occasional chirp of crickets. Fireflies flickered around the water, blending in with the sea of tiny flames floating in the lake.

Luke grinned at her as he took her hand and led her down to the shore. He must've gotten someone to help him pull off a feat like this, and Geneva was stunned. He managed to surprise her, and not necessarily in a bad way.

"It's beautiful, isn't it?" he asked, helping her climb into the rowboat. "A lake isn't quite as awesome as the ocean, but it works better for my purposes. Besides, look how many stars you can see way out here."

He gestured up to the night sky, so packed with stars that the whole lake was cast in a silvery, gleaming light. When he began to point out the constellations, Geneva felt a strong stirring in her chest, a warm affection that almost seemed to burst her heart open. She really loved Luke and how sweet he was. She made the right choice when she chose him out of all the other men she could have chosen on Earth.

They took the boat out into the middle of the lake, where everything around them was radiant and serene, the sound of the oars sloshing through the water.

"This is where I would have proposed to you," he explained, though Geneva already had the inkling. "I'm sorry I couldn't wait."

"I'm glad you didn't, Luke. I like knowing how much you want to be with me."

He smiled at her in a way that made her insides feel like jelly.

"I'm glad you want to be my wife," he replied. "I can't wait to start my life with you."

He leaned across the distance between them and kissed her innocently on the mouth. Then he reached for the blanket beneath her seat and wrapped it around her shoulders, making sure it was nice and snug. He popped open the bottle of champagne and grabbed some flutes from beneath his own seat, pouring each of them a glass, and they cheered to the future of their marriage.

It was a moment of sheer bliss for Geneva, who had waited for so long for this to happen. All the work and effort she had put into the relationship had finally paid off.

They spent the rest of the evening on the rowboat, drinking champagne and basking under the stars.

* * *

Geneva had a permanent smile on her face in the days following Luke's proposal. She couldn't have been happier if she tried, and though they still hadn't tied the knot, things were beginning to feel *final.*

The first bump in the road didn't come until Luke insisted that she meet his cousin, Lindsey. It was long overdue, of course. Usually, she would have met the family of her future husband *before* she agreed to marry him. He had met Eugenia several times already, after all, and that was all that really mattered to Geneva.

She wasn't much of a family person, though she knew that Luke absolutely was. That made it much harder to reject him when he invited her to come to dinner with him and Lindsey. She couldn't be sure that Lindsey wouldn't remember her as her fake persona, Veronica. It was possible Geneva could pass it off as a mere resemblance, but she had to tread carefully. Lindsey wasn't exactly stupid, and she had been suspicious even when they first met.

That day, Geneva did her make up a little differently, contouring a little less and applying a little more blush. She pulled her hair back into a messy bun rather than keeping it loose around her shoulder like she usually did, and hoped it would be enough to fool Lindsey.

She arrived at the restaurant after the two of them had already been seated, and she walked up to the table with a fake smile plastered on her face.

"Geneva," Luke said warmly, rising to greet her with a kiss on the cheek. "This is my cousin, Lindsey."

Luke pulled out Geneva's chair as she shook Lindsey's hand. There was a strange silence that settled over the table as she sat down and unfolded her napkin.

"You look familiar," Lindsey said, tapping her finger against her lips. "Do I know you?"

Geneva shrugged, feigning indifference. "I'm not sure," she replied.

Lindsey gave her a disbelieving look, but said nothing else until the waiter arrived to take their orders. Luke tried to make polite chitchat between the three of them, but his efforts were in vain since neither Lindsey nor Geneva were all that interested in each other.

Geneva knew that her reason was jealousy and fear of being outed. She had no clue why Lindsey didn't seem to like her. She was suspicious of something, but Geneva couldn't tell what it was. It made her nervous throughout dinner, unsure of how to act.

Luke seemed to pick up on the tension between the two of them. He tilted his head at the both of them throughout dinner, a little skeptical and a little wary. It was one of the most uncomfortably awkward dinners Geneva had ever sat through.

On the way back home, Luke brought it up to her.

"That seemed pretty weird, didn't it?" he asked as they walked home hand-in-hand.

Geneva gave a nonchalant shrug.

"Neither of you said more than five words to each other the entire dinner," he said with exasperation. "I really thought the two of you would get along."

Geneva brushed off the concerns, assuring him that she had nothing against his cousin, and they would get along just fine. He still seemed worried about it that night when they went to bed. *She* couldn't help but be worried about it. Lindsey was Luke's closest family member. She *had* to get along with Lindsey, or she, at least, had to make a deal with Lindsey to not say anything about her uncouth moment as Veronica.

That meant coming up with another plan. She thought she would be done with all this nonsense once she had the ring on her finger, but it occurred to her as she slipped into bed that night and settled her head against his chest that, from now on, it would be a constant struggle to keep her vampirism a secret from him.

***

Geneva was hesitant to meet the rest of Luke's family. Her less than warm welcome from Lindsey seemed indicative of how they would feel by extension. Geneva had looked through all the social media pages of every family member of his that she knew of and found that many of them had known about Holly.

In public, they posted comments lamenting her absence. In private, when Geneva logged into Luke's accounts, she found scathing comments in his messages from family members wondering what he had done to drive off a sweet girl like Holly. If she weren't so panicked, she would have been angry that Luke found it in himself to introduce Holly to his family so early on into their short-lived relationship.

Geneva had the kind of predator magnetism that made men like her, but it didn't make mothers or families like her. She was afraid she might disappoint his family and put a wedge between her and Luke. So, she made excuses to avoid them, did everything possible not to include them in the wedding plans.

Of course, it drove a wedge between them anyway. Luke's family was so important to him, and she could see it bothered him that she didn't seem to want anything to do with them.

And that wasn't the only thing he was bothered by. One night, he had come home with the battery on his cell phone dead. He plugged it in and asked Geneva if he could use hers to make a quick work call. She thought nothing of it when she handed the phone over, but as soon as he saw his own social media pages pulled up on the screen, he became withdrawn.

Geneva knew he had seen them, but he said nothing about it. He made his work call in the room with her and then hung up, passed the phone back to her, and went straight upstairs into the bedroom.

***

For a few days after that, things between them were tense. Neither of them brought it up, but she could tell that Luke was angry with her. She didn't entirely blame him, but he didn't know that she was doing all this for his own good.

The next straw for Luke was when Lindsey refused to be his "best man" for the wedding. During a phone conversation on which Geneva had eavesdropped, she learned that Lindsey thought there was something off about Geneva and couldn't condone the marriage. She wanted Luke to reconsider, or at least, give it a little more time.

Geneva wasn't sure there was anything she could do about that. She briefly toyed with the idea of killing Lindsey, but that would only hurt Luke in the long run.

When Luke finally found the courage to confront her about things, he sat her down in the living room, his expression stony and serious.

"Geneva," he began softly. "We need to talk."

She said nothing, afraid of incriminating herself.

"You've been spying on me," he asserted, swallowing a lump in his throat. "After I saw my social media on your phone, I checked my computer. I saw the browser history. I know what you've been doing. My schedule. My bank account. My emails. You've been keeping tabs on me. Why?"

Geneva blinked, trying to stop the vomit threatening to come up. He didn't sound angry, but he sounded suspicious and a little scared. She would much rather have him be angry with her, an emotion she could deal with.

It would've been so much easier to lose Luke if he were never really hers to begin with.

"Why, Geneva?" he pressed when she remained silent. "I've been loyal to you. I've never done anything to make you doubt me."

"No, you haven't," she said softly. "It's not that."

"Then what is it?"

"I just..."

Luke let out a sigh of impatience and rubbed his forehead. Then he smoothed his hands together and clasped his fingers with the practiced charisma of a kindergarten teacher.

"Geneva, spit it out."

"It just makes me feel better," she explained, her breath shaky. "I like knowing what's going on with you."

He gave her a scathing look. "My bank account? Come on, Geneva, you know that's crazy. If there's something you wanted to know, you could just ask me. The only thing I ever hid from you was buying the engagement ring, but you knew about that anyway, didn't you?"

"Oh, really?" she asked, her tone raising. "So, you didn't try to hide Holly from me?"

Luke flinched. "Why would I need to hide her? She has nothing to do with you."

"You started seeing her after our first date," she pointed out, crossing her arms over her chest. It felt good to have a little bit of high ground to stand on.

"We weren't exclusive then, and I apologized for my behavior."

Geneva glared at him, clenching her teeth until her jaw hurt.

"What do you want from me, Geneva? Holly's gone. She's not even in the picture anymore."

"But you wish she was, don't you?"

He looked ashamed, but a fiery anger was back in his eyes in an instant. "There's nothing I can do about that," he yelled as tears formed in his eyes. "Unless you're suggesting that I should be chasing after her. If you're worried I'd leave you for her, I would *never* do that. You are the woman I asked to marry me. That's why I don't understand all the spying."

"Yeah, I'm not worried about that," Geneva said, looking away from him. Her mixed emotions were stirring up her thirst, making her fangs protrude. She wouldn't be able to continue this conversation until she could get herself under control.

"What's that supposed to mean?" Luke asked.

Geneva sighed and kept her gaze fixed on a spot on the carpet between her feet.

"You had something to do with her ghosting me, didn't you?" he demanded, rising up to his feet.

Now, he was angry, but Geneva wasn't sure how to counter it. This was exactly what she feared, and now that it was happening, she felt like she deserved it.

Her mind went to Michael. Patient and understanding Michael. He liked being around her, spending time with her. With him, she never had to try so hard. Even when she was herself, even when she disappointed him, Michael still wanted to be her friend.

As someone without many friends, Geneva really valued that. She had worked so hard to get Luke, and now in an instant, she had lost him.

"Answer me, Geneva," he shouted.

"I'm so sorry, Luke," Geneva said sincerely. "I never wanted to hurt you. I only wanted what's best for you."

The glare he sent her pierced straight through her heart.

"You wanted what's best for *you*."

"Luke—"

"Give me my ring back," he said, extending his palm. When she didn't move, he snapped his fingers until she reluctantly removed the ring, fighting back a wave of tears. She held the diamond clenched in her fist for a moment before she hesitantly placed it in his open palm. He closed his hand and then pointed to the door.

"Now, get out of my house."

"You can't be serious, Luke. Where am I supposed to go?"

"I don't give a fuck where you go."

Geneva swallowed her tears, giving her best effort to keep the trembling out of her voice. She knew how weak and pathetic she sounded, but she couldn't help it.

"I thought you loved me."

Luke gave her a roving look, eyeing her with disdain. His expression softened just sightly when his gaze landed on her face.

"Lindsey was right about you."

Geneva blinked. She took a few deep, steadying breaths before she calmly stood up and retrieved her purse. She walked to the front door and put her hand on the knob.

"Goodbye, Luke," she said.

He didn't say a word to her, but she could hear the quickness of his pulse when she shut the front door behind her.

Chapter Fourteen

The doorbell at Eugenia's house was broken, so Geneva had to pull aside the massive wreath of fake flowers and pumpkins to knock. She waited for a moment and knocked again, trying to keep her eyes dry, at least until she got inside.

When the door swung open, it was Parker standing there instead of Eugenia, dressed in faded khakis and a baggy polo shirt. The urge to wrinkle her nose in disgust compelled her not to cry so she could speak.

"Is Eugenia here?"

"In the shower," Parker said, opening the door wider for her. "Come in, sit down. You look awful. Is everything alright?"

Geneva stared at him as she entered the house and dropped her purse onto the entryway table. Parker was a boring, blustering man, but every now and then, Geneva saw what her sister saw in him. He was peering at her with genuine concern as he led her into the living room.

"I'm fine. I just need to talk to Eugenia."

Parker nodded at her as she sat down on the couch. She wasn't prone to dropping by unannounced, so he knew it had to be something serious. Geneva kept her left hand in the palm of her right, hiding her empty ring finger as he disappeared around the corner.

She heard his thudding footsteps go up the stairs. In the silence, she could hear the water in the shower running. Geneva listened to their muffled conversation over the running water, unable to understand most of it. The faucet squeaked, and the flow of water stopped. Geneva waited anxiously, eager to cry but not until she had explained everything to Eugenia.

If the breakup wasn't bad enough, it was humiliating to have nowhere to go. She didn't even want to think about having to go back to get all her things, to find a new place to live, or begin to think of what to do next.

She wanted to wallow in her misery, but it made her feel guilty to inflict that on her sister. As Eugenia walked into the room in a bathrobe and her hair up in a towel, Geneva swallowed the lump in her throat and closed her eyes for composure.

"Geneva, what's wrong?" Eugenia asked, rushing to her side.

Geneva felt her weight dip into the couch, the cushion bouncing beneath it. She looked at her sister and opened her mouth to speak.

No words came out. Instead, the sobs that she had been holding in all unleashed. Hot tears spilled down her cheeks, and her desperate wails of heartache echoed throughout the house. Eugenia wrapped her arms around her, and they sat down on the couch, Geneva sobbing into her sister's shoulder.

"Geneva, tell me what happened," Eugenia said, her voice filled with concern.

"Luke broke up with me," she wept through her sobs.

Eugenia's hand came down on her shoulder to rub soothing circles there. She had the practiced and controlled movements of someone who had handled crying many times before. Eugenia had a natural and maternal empathy that made her one of Geneva's favorite people, despite how annoying she found her most of the time.

"You can stay here as long as you need," Eugenia assured her.

She didn't ask about the breakup, and Geneva hated that she could practically feel the judgement coming off her sister in waves. This was just one more failed relationship to tally onto the wall.

It wasn't like she *wanted* to stay with Eugenia and her husband. It was humiliating.

"Parker, can you set up the guest bedroom for her?" Eugenia asked softly over Geneva's shoulder.

He obediently shuffled away, and Geneva wondered if maybe she should just settle for some guy like Parker instead.

She *could* do that, she realized. With Michael. He wasn't quite the Prince Charming she had envisioned in her mind, but he loved her and cared about her. He would treat her well, and his feelings would be reciprocated instead of forced.

With Michael, she wouldn't have to worry. She wouldn't have to make plans, or spy, or lose herself in an obsession over him.

"Am I hopeless?" Geneva asked, her voice muffled by Eugenia's shoulder.

"No, you're not hopeless," Eugenia insisted.

"Do you think I'll ever find the kind of love that you have?"

Eugenia's hand faltered where it smoothed over Geneva's back. She knew her sister wasn't used to her being so open and vulnerable.

"I think you'll find love when you're ready for it, Geneva," Eugenia said.

That was the kind of flowery and vague statement Geneva used to appease her patients, so she wasn't blind to the comforting effect of it. How does someone even ready themselves for love?

"How about I put on some re-runs of The Bachelor?" Eugenia suggested. "I'll make Parker run to the grocery store and get us some mint chocolate chip ice cream."

Geneva nodded, eager for a distraction.

"And some rocky road," she added.

***

Geneva wasted no time in signing a lease on a new apartment and getting back to work. She was still absolutely crushed, but outwardly, she managed to pull herself together. It had been cathartic to cry on her sister's couch, but the wallowing got old quickly.

But now, she had to focus on getting her life back together. She couldn't rely on Luke to love her anymore, and she had officially ended her obsession with him. She thought she could love him forever, but she was wrong. It wasn't the first time she had been wrong about a man.

After work, she headed home to her apartment rather than stopping by the coffee corner. Now that Luke had broken up with her, she had conflicted feelings about Michael. She always knew he was attracted to her, but she had made it pretty clear early on that she was never going to reciprocate those feelings.

She couldn't just tease and flirt to win him over now. He would think that was cruel. She had to do the one thing she hated doing. Be vulnerable. She would have to confess her feelings for Michael and deal with the impossibly painful idea that he might reject her. It would be devastating to be rejected by Michael right after losing Luke. She didn't want him to think he was a rebound for her either.

So, Geneva did the most logical thing and avoided him entirely. She grew tired of it quickly. She missed him, especially now that she had no one to complain to about her life. She was already ashamed of the side of herself she had shown to Eugenia.

But that meant she was confined to her tiny apartment by herself. She had no one to talk to, no friends to speak of. Every now and then, she walked past Meat & Greet and glanced through the window to see Michael behind the counter. He always seemed to be in a good mood, which made her feel angry for reasons she didn't know.

Work became unbearably hard because of her emotions. She couldn't focus on her patients, nor muster up any urge to care about any of it. She took some time away from the office and planned a getaway trip to the beach.

She had planned to be gone for several months in attempts to better herself and muster up the courage to confess her feelings to Michael in a healthy way.

Only as she was packing for her trip, she realized that she didn't want to spend that time away from him. She didn't want to spend more time alone than she already had. It would be better to lay everything out into the open now and hope for the best.

Her instincts told her to find Michael when he was outside of work so they could have this discussion in private, but the only method she knew of for doing that was snooping. She was determined to do this the right way with Michael, so instead of resorting to stalking again, she sucked it up and met him at his place of work.

He looked happy but surprised to see her when she walked up to the counter. There was a sympathetic glimmer in his eyes, and she suspected that he already knew about her breakup with Luke. Probably from Luke himself.

"Hey, Geneva," he said warmly. "It's been a while."

"Too long," Geneva agreed. "Listen, I was wondering if I could talk to you. Later. In private."

"More… vampire stuff?" he whispered, leaning close to her face over the counter. The action sent the sweet tang of his blood through the air between them.

Geneva shook her head. "Something else."

Michael gave her a confused look and then his expression grew serious and concerned. "Is everything alright?" he asked. "I was sorry to hear about your breakup."

She didn't know how to feel about the fact that he genuinely seemed sorry for her, or the fact that he even knew about the breakup. Geneva swallowed the lump in her throat and shook her head again. "It's not about that either," she explained. "Please. I'll tell you tonight. My apartment?"

He gave her a doubtful look. "You aren't going to kill me, are you?"

"Michael! I would never do that."

"I'm teasing, Geneva," he said with a disarming grin. "I know you wouldn't."

She let out a chuckle of relief and tucked a lock of hair behind her ear. The line behind her was starting to get long, so Geneva gave him her address and asked him to come over after his shift ended. She left without ordering anything and went straight home.

At home, she cleaned and took a shower, then she found an old bottle of whiskey from the back of her pantry and took a few swigs to calm her nerves.

She tried to come up with a script, tried to put her feelings into words so it wouldn't be so hard to do it in front of Michael. After all this time, despite her anxiety about telling him, she felt certain that what she felt for Michael was *real*.

With the other men, particularly Luke, the obsession had been about the *idea* of who they could be, especially under her control.

But she didn't want to control Michael. She just wanted him to love her, and on his own volition, without her meddling. It was a relief to finally feel that way about someone, and to understand where she had gone wrong in all her other relationships.

She understood now what Eugenia had been trying to tell her. She had brushed it off as pettiness and Eugenia's eternal habit for being a busybody. But she was right. Eugenia had been right this whole time.

A sharp knock at the door brought her out of her head and back into the chilly air in her apartment living room. Trembling, she walked to the door and swung it open.

"Good evening," Michael said cautiously, still a little unsure of why he was here.

"Hey, Michael. Come in."

Geneva ushered him into the living room and sat him down on the couch. She offered him a drink, which he declined. She wanted to take another shot of whiskey, but she knew she'd quickly get sick if she did.

"Michael, I have something I want to tell you," she said. "I'm just going to say it quick so I can get it over with and not mess it up."

He cocked his head to the side, his face a mixture of confusion and nervousness.

"I love you," she said. "This whole time, I have been obsessed with Luke, but *you* were the one I could never stop thinking about. *You* were the one who helped me, who kept me sane. You're one of the few people on Earth that I actually like to be around, and well… I guess I'm saying, I want to be around you all the time."

A silence settled over the room. Michael's brow was furrowed with confusion, his dark eyes piercing and severe. The look sent dread flowing through her stomach, her worst fear realized.

"I'm just a barista," he said. "Are you sure you want to be with a lowly coffee slave?"

It stung to have that thrown back in her face, but she knew she deserved it.

"I wouldn't care if you were a street magician or a lawyer, Michael," she said. "I just want to be with you. And I'm sorry it took me so long to figure it out."

Reluctantly, a small smile came to his face.

"I *did* always have a crush on you," he said.

"Yeah, I know."

"It really hurt to see you chasing after Luke like that."

"I know," she repeated, nodding in understanding. "You warned me about what would happen, and I didn't listen to you. That seems to be a theme in my life."

"Geneva, deep down you are a compassionate person," Michael said, taking her hand in his and resting both on his lap.

She repressed a shiver and met his gaze.

"I think you feel a lot of guilt," he continued. "You know, you can be cruel sometimes, but it's only because you have to constantly fight a monster inside you. You're not that person, and you never have been. You've stopped killing people, haven't you?"

She nodded, thinking of the empty blood bags overflowing in the dumpster out back.

"It's impressive to see you battle with it and win," he praised. "You're strong, Geneva. That's what I've always liked about you. Sometimes I envy your strength, and especially your ambition. You always go right after what you want."

He looked away. His hand sweaty around her fingers.

"You've taught me a lot, too," he continued softly.

Then he looked back up into her eyes, his dark lashes fanning over his cheeks as he blinked. He wore an expression of pure longing and adoration, a look that tugged on the corners of Geneva's soul.

He closed the distance between them and kissed her, his hands flying up to cup her neck with gentle, reverent fingers. The kiss was naïve but warm and tender, just a simple show of affection. Though the touch was light, Geneva could hear the quick pounding of his heart, and this time, when her fangs came out, she didn't have to hide her face as she pulled away.

Michael panted as he stared at her mouth, his cheeks flushed with color. Whether his eyes were on her lips or fangs, she couldn't be sure.

He kissed her again, this time, a little less modestly. When he started to deepen it, his blood rushing and fingers trembling, Geneva pushed him away with a gentle hand on his chest.

"Stop," she murmured. "I don't want to hurt you."

"Did you ever hurt Luke?"

She flicked her gaze away from him, trying to quell her pounding heart and the bloodlust forcing her fangs out of her gums.

"Not like that," she said breathlessly, "but it was hard, you know. I had to leave the room sometimes."

Michael nodded. "I remember that," he said. "You don't have to leave the room now."

"I suppose not," she said softly.

Silence settled over them again, though this time, it was far more comfortable. Michael had a sweet, endearing smile on his face. He leaned back against the couch, at ease in her home, at her side, in front of her fangs. It was nice to have someone she could be her real self around.

"So, are you my girlfriend now?" he asked after a moment had passed.

Geneva chuckled. "Yeah, I am."

"Should I hand over my bank statements or what?"

She slapped him on the shoulder and glared at him even though she knew he was just teasing. "It should go without saying, but I'm done doing all the secretive, manipulative stuff," she explained.

"I know," he replied. "I wouldn't be here otherwise."

She looked at him and gave him a nod of approval. "Good."

"Oh, and I love you, too, by the way," he said.

Geneva smiled. "You do?"

"I have for a while," he confessed. "Especially after you opened up to me about being a vampire. I'm glad I was able to earn your trust. It sounds silly, but it's a very powerful feeling. And you can trust me with it because I love you."

Even though her fangs hadn't quite receded just yet, Geneva couldn't resist the urge to pull him into another kiss.

"I think we should take a trip somewhere," she suggested when they broke apart.

"Where?" he asked.

"Anywhere," she replied. "I just want to leave this place for a while."

"How about a road trip?" he offered.

Geneva broke into a wide grin, excited by the idea. Usually, she would find the prospect of a long car ride insufferable, but she would be happy anywhere with Michael by her side.

"Yes, absolutely," she agreed. "Go home, and pack your bags, then meet me back here. We can take my car."

Michael laughed. "Woah, slow down," he said. "I have to ask for time off work. I can't just up and leave."

"Call in sick," she urged. "Please. I want to leave tonight."

"Tomorrow," he bartered. "We both need to get a good night's sleep first."

"Fine," she said reluctantly. "Then you'll meet me back here first thing in the morning?"

"First thing in the morning," he agreed.

***

True to his word, Michael was at her door early the next morning, before the sun had even come up. Bleary eyed and still dressed in her pajamas, she let him inside. She got herself dressed while he loaded their things up into her car.

She felt a sense of belonging as she slid into the passenger seat and glanced over at Michael. He looked at ease and comfortable in her car, and braced his arm over the back of her seat to turn and look as he backed out of the driveway.

"This is going to be so much fun," Geneva predicted. "We can drive down to Florida and go to the beach. We can pass through the Smoky Mountains. Anywhere we want to go."

"Let's just see where the wind takes us," he suggested.

The both of them were eager and giddy when they hit the early morning road, the sun barely visible in a thin line on the horizon. Geneva admired the colors in the sky as they drove through green trees and rolling hills.

It gave her a sense of purpose to be on the road with him. She longed for this kind of freedom and love. Nothing had ever felt this good in her entire life – not even Luke's admittedly romantic proposal. It was the most content she had ever felt, and she wondered about all the moments she had been missing out on because she couldn't learn to control her obsessions.

Michael had a calmness and surety about him that made him feel safe for her. He kept asking her silly questions as they drove, like what her favorite snacks were and what kind of music she liked to listen to. She indulged him in the light-hearted conversation, realizing that she knew very little about him.

Hopefully, this trip would remedy that. The first tidbit of information she tucked away was his love for boring political talk radio.

Barely an hour on the road, the rumble of the car against the pavement and the drone of Michael's talk radio made her drowsy. Geneva rolled onto her side, faced the window, and fell asleep.

***

She woke up with a sour taste in her mouth. Her eyes were crusted shut, and a horrible nausea filled her stomach. She fluttered her eyes, wincing against the bright fluorescent lighting above. Her head was absolutely pounding, her eyes swollen and puffy.

"Oh, thank God," she heard a familiar voice sigh as she sat up against the soft pillows behind her.

She was in a hospital room, wrapped in a thin paper gown beneath a scratchy blanket.

Eugenia sat beside her, leaning in close over the bed; her brows were scrunched with worry. She gripped Geneva's hands with white knuckles, her pulse quick.

"What happened?" Geneva groaned, rubbing at the tenderness of her temples.

"You were in a car accident," Eugenia said. "It was bad, Geneva. A helicopter had to airlift you to the closest hospital. You almost didn't make it. In fact, no one is even sure how you're still alive. You've been out for days."

Confused, Geneva looked around the room and swallowed. The window showed a familiar cityscape, and the sky was mockingly dark. She couldn't remember anything about the accident or how she got to the hospital.

"I don't understand," she said, looking to her sister for help.

"A truck rolled over a bridge on the interstate," Eugenia explained. "It landed on your car and nearly killed you."

Panic seized Geneva's heart. "Michael," she said desperately. "Is he okay? Where is he?"

Eugenia gave her a somber look and shook her head. "I'm so sorry, Geneva," she said softly, her voice barely above a whisper.

Geneva vigorously shook her head, the effort making her head ache. "No," she rasped, trying to swing her legs over the side of the bed to get up. Eugenia held her back and easily pushed her weak body onto the bed.

"He was killed instantly, Geneva," Eugenia said. "He didn't suffer."

Hot tears slipped from her eyes, her heart constricting painfully in her chest. How could she have let this happen? This was all her fault. She had been the one to suggest the sudden road trip, and now, Michael was dead because of it.

"I have to get out of here," Geneva said, anxiety swelling in her chest. She tried to stand up again, but Eugenia wouldn't let her.

"You're still hurt," she argued. "You have to get some rest and heal before they'd let you leave. So just sit down and relax."

Compliant, Geneva sank back against her pillow and let out a nervous, uncertain sigh.

"He's dead because of me," she said out loud.

Eugenia shook her head. "No, that's not true."

"He's dead because I was selfish," Geneva insisted, "because I wanted to spend more time with him. I wanted to be with him after all this time, all that energy wasted on Luke. And now, he's just gone. What am I supposed to do now, Eugenia? How do I keep messing things up this badly?" She collapsed into her sister's arms, weeping uncontrollably.

"Oh, sis, none of this is your fault," Eugenia replied, rubbing her arm soothingly. "You can't blame yourself for the accident."

Geneva *did* blame herself for the accident, but not just that. She held a lot of blame for a number of things she'd done over the years. She thought she could spend the rest of her life atoning with Michael, who seemed to have been the only person to truly understand her.

Eugenia stayed by her side until she fell asleep again, though sleep came fitfully and unreliably through the night. She was gone when Geneva finally woke up, so Geneva yanked the tubes and needles out of her body and snuck her way out of the hospital. It wasn't safe for her to be there, hooked up to their machines.

Outside the hospital, she hailed a cab. She glanced at the man in the driver's seat before she slid into the back of the car. She didn't know where to go, but she knew she needed a fresh start, somewhere no one knew her name.

"Where are we headed?" he asked.

"Anywhere," Geneva replied. "As long as it's far away from here."

Fatal Kiss

Fatal Kiss